BEWITCHING WINTER

by

SERENITY WOODS

Copyright © 2016 Serenity Woods
All rights reserved.
ISBN: 1537173375
ISBN-13: 978-1537173375

DEDICATION

To Tony & Chris, my Kiwi boys.

CONTENTS

Chapter One 1
Chapter Two 10
Chapter Three 17
Chapter Four 24
Chapter Five 31
Chapter Six 38
Chapter Seven 45
Chapter Eight 52
Chapter Nine 59
Chapter Ten 66
Chapter Eleven 72
Chapter Twelve 79
Chapter Thirteen 85
Chapter Fourteen 91
Chapter Fifteen 98
Chapter Sixteen 105
Chapter Seventeen 111
Chapter Eighteen 117
Chapter Nineteen 124
Chapter Twenty 131
Chapter Twenty-One 138
Chapter Twenty-Two 146
Chapter Twenty-Three 152
Chapter Twenty-Four 160
Chapter Twenty-Five 166
Chapter Twenty-Six 175
Epilogue 182
The Four Seasons 186
About the Author 187

Chapter One

Neve was tired.

Unfortunately, that wasn't anything new. For several years now, she'd been suffering from insomnia, which had led to her being permanently exhausted, distracted, and irritable.

Of course, it was possible she was just irritable by nature. She honestly couldn't remember a time when she hadn't been tired, so it was kind of difficult to say.

She'd never been the sort of person to sleep for more than five or six hours anyway, so she'd trained herself to exist on little sleep. As a teenager, and even in her early twenties, she'd worked hard and partied harder, and then she'd dated Rhett, and he'd kept her up most of the night for other, sexier reasons. After they'd broken up, she'd spent a few years trying to regain the carefree abandon of her youth, but lately the appeal of parties and late nights had waned. It didn't mean she got more sleep though. It just meant that midnight was more likely to find her in bed with a cup of hot chocolate and a good book than dancing in a nightclub. In the past any lack of sleep wouldn't have mattered, but now it seemed to be taking its toll.

God, she was getting old.

She hadn't slept a wink the night before. Her doctor had said that insomniacs got more sleep than they thought and that she must doze lightly without realizing it, but each time she'd rolled over and glanced at the hotel alarm clock she'd found that barely ten minutes had passed, until eventually the sky had begun to lighten and she'd felt justified in dragging herself out of bed and into the shower.

Not only was it Monday morning, it was also mid-June, three days from the winter solstice in the southern hemisphere, the absolute worst time for a summer-adoring, bikini-loving girl to have taken herself off to the South Island of New Zealand, to the snowy landscape of Queenstown. Booking a marketing course had seemed like a great idea back in April. Now she'd rather be doing anything than sitting in a conference room with a hundred people who thought themselves entrepreneurs and would no doubt bore her rigid with detailed stories of how they'd come to run their own businesses.

Grouchily, she made her way down to the foyer for breakfast, half debating whether she should just walk straight out of the front door and head home. One of the conference organizers lay in wait for unsuspecting attendees, however, and gave her a welcome pack for her to digest along with her cereal and orange juice.

Stifling a groan, she crossed the tiled foyer, then stopped as her phone vibrated in her pocket. She took it out and looked at the screen, and her heart sank. It was her sister, Deana.

Her finger hovered over the red button, and then she sighed, swiped the screen, and answered. "Hello?"

"It's me," Deana said. "Are you at the hotel?"

"Yeah, about to go in for breakfast. You're early. What's up?" It had to be some kind of catastrophe. Deana only ever rang when a disaster hovered on the horizon.

"Nothing's up. I spoke to Mum yesterday, that's all."

Neve studied her fingernails. "How is she?"

"She's good. Missing you, though."

"I sent her an email on Friday."

"I know. It's not the same as seeing you though, is it?"

"I told her I'm happy to meet her for a coffee in town any time she wants."

"Neve… How long are you going to keep this up? It's been six months."

"Don't start."

Deana sighed. "Just go around there and get it over with. Say you're sorry for walking out. You don't have to mean it. You know Dad will never say it, and all the time you carry on like this you're making everyone miserable."

Neve gave a short, harsh laugh. "*I'm* making everyone miserable? You were there, Dee, you heard what he said."

"I know… It was awful. I still can't believe he'd say something like that. But it's just his way. I'm sure he thought he might shock you into…"

"Into what?" Neve said icily.

Deana cleared her throat. "I don't know. Look, he doesn't understand how speaking his mind can hurt people's feelings."

"That's because he doesn't have any."

"He does, and you've hurt his by refusing to go around there."

"I don't care." Neve spoke flatly. "I'm done with him. All my life I've had to put up with his criticism. You don't understand because you're his favorite, but he's always picked on me. I'm tired of feeling as if I can never do anything right, and I'm not going to sit there and be insulted like that. He thinks he can say what he wants to the women in his life and they'll just kowtow to him, but I'm sick of it."

"I don't kowtow." Defensiveness sharpened Deana's tone. "But there's no point in arguing with him because he won't listen. I learned that long ago. I'd rather just say 'Yes, Dad' and then go and do my own thing. He's not winning that way, Neve."

"But he thinks he is! And that's what matters, don't you understand?"

"So… what? You're trying to teach him a lesson?"

"Maybe. He can't treat us all like doormats. It's wrong, and I'm not going to put up with it just to keep the peace."

"Even if it's making Mum unhappy? She's so sad, Neve. She cried while I was talking to her."

Neve's throat tightened, but she refused to give in. "I'm sorry to hear that, but it's partly her fault. If she'd said no to him occasionally throughout their marriage, maybe he wouldn't be like he is now."

"Please don't be like this. You're just hurting Mum and making it more difficult for all of us."

"I've got to go," Neve snapped.

"Neve—"

She hung up and slid the phone back into her pocket.

For a moment, she couldn't move, her chest heaving with indignation, her jaw clenched tight. Her father still treated her as if she were thirteen, thinking he could pass judgment on her life, believing he knew what was best for her. She was sure that, in itself, wasn't unusual—most fathers were probably the same. But his words to her the last time they'd met had been seared into her brain, and she couldn't erase them no matter how hard she tried.

It had been Christmas Day. Her mother, Bella, had invited everyone around in an attempt—Neve was sure—to reinstate some of the family closeness that had been lacking for a while. Bella had gone to great effort to cook a roast dinner with all the trimmings, as if the quality of the food would somehow help to stave off the impending doom they'd all felt. Deana and her husband, Jamie, had been there with their two-year-old daughter, and Neve had seen them exchange a look of *Uh-oh, told you,* when Brian Clark had asked Neve how her boyfriend, Simon, was.

"We broke up." She'd helped herself to the buttered carrots. He'd been picking on her since she'd arrived, and she was losing patience.

Brian had given a humorless laugh. "Jesus."

"Don't swear," her mother had muttered.

"There must be something seriously wrong with you." Brian had stabbed at a piece of roast turkey. "You can't hold down a relationship for more than six weeks."

Don't bite, Neve had warned herself, but she'd gripped her knife and fork and sawn with some venom at a roast potato. "That's not quite true," she'd said as mildly as she could.

"Dad…" Deana had begun hesitantly.

"You're stubborn and outspoken," he'd continued, ignoring Deana. "It's no wonder you can't keep a man for longer than it takes him to get you into bed. Maybe if you acted like a lady and closed your mouth and your legs once in a while, you'd have more luck."

Deana had gasped. Jamie's eyebrows had disappeared into his hairline. Bella had covered her face with her hand.

Neve had put down her knife and fork, picked up her handbag and car keys, and walked out. She hadn't been back since.

Leaning against a pillar in the foyer, once again she considered turning on her heel and heading home. Then she set her jaw. She wasn't going to let anyone or anything ruin this. She'd come here to escape and to concentrate on her business. Screw everyone else.

Lifting her chin, she walked a little way into the restaurant, pondering on whether she felt like a full English breakfast, and then her gaze fell on two men standing talking by the coffee pot. She stopped and inhaled sharply. No. Surely not.

She knew one of them. About a week ago, when she'd seen him at a bar in Wellington, he'd worn jeans, a T-shirt, and trainers. Today he'd donned a navy suit and a crisp white shirt with a blue-and-gray striped tie and smart black shoes. She'd never seen him in a suit, but she was certain it was him.

Fuck.

As if he could feel her stare boring into his back like a laser, he turned and looked straight at her. Their gazes met and locked, turning her to stone.

For a long moment, Neve couldn't catch her breath. She'd seen him many times over the last eighteen months or so since he'd returned to Wellington, but it shocked her to see him here, in Queenstown. Anger flooded her, white hot. She was here on business. She'd come away to try to get her life back on track. How dare he intrude when he was the cause of all her problems in the first place!

Her resentment must have shown on her face, because he glanced at the floor briefly, and she thought she saw him give a small sigh. He looked up and smiled at the man next to him and said something, and then he started to walk across the restaurant toward her.

Neve turned away, heart racing, wanting to march straight out of the hotel, get in a taxi, and head for the airport. She didn't want to see him, didn't want to talk to him, didn't even want to think about him. Perhaps he just happened to be staying at the hotel, she tried to reassure herself, and he'd be heading off soon, but she knew it was too much of a coincidence. He worked as a marketing consultant—naturally he'd be there to attend the marketing and promotion course.

Her feet itched to move, but stubbornness made her stand still. She wasn't going to let him scare her away. She had as much right to be there as he did.

"Neve." His voice sounded from behind her.

Taking a deep breath, she turned and looked up at him. "Hi, Rhett."

For a long moment, neither of them said anything. Did looking at her transport him back to when they'd first met at Willow's wedding, the way it did whenever she looked at him? He'd changed a lot since then, though. His body had filled out, losing the slender leanness of youth and taking on the muscular build of a man. Whereas he'd hardly ever bothered to shave back then, now his jaw was smooth enough to make her fingers itch to touch it. Back then, he'd had a buzz cut, but now his hair was longer and just-got-out-of-bed ruffled, although she wasn't sure if it was natural or if he'd styled it that way.

His eyes were still the same interesting shade of hazel, though, changing from brown to green with his mood. He still possessed more charisma in his little finger than most men had in their entire bodies. And, even after all these years, when he looked at her a tingle still ran down her spine as sure as if he'd reached around and trailed a finger down her back.

"Long time no see," he said.

"We saw each other last week," she pointed out. "At the bar."

"Long time no speak, then," he clarified.

She gave a small nod. Even though he occasionally joined their group of friends when they went out on a Friday night, they'd hardly exchanged two words since they'd broken up. For the first few years he'd been abroad, and he'd not made the effort to contact her once during that time. She hadn't attempted to get in touch either, but his lack of communication had hurt her almost as much as the break up. The first time she'd seen him on his return to Wellington, he'd tried to talk to her, but she'd told him in no uncertain terms that nothing had changed since he'd gone away, and she had nothing to say to him. Since then, she'd studiously avoided meeting his eyes or talking to him, and she made sure she was never, ever, alone with him.

"Are you here for the course?" she asked.

"Yeah."

"Right." She looked toward the foyer. It would be so simple to nip up, collect her bags from the room, and just walk out. She'd been thinking about leaving anyway. It would be awful if she stayed. She'd be conscious of him in the room the whole time, and she wouldn't be able to relax. Plus she knew the course involved working in groups—what if they were put together? How could she stand being near him?

"I hear Four Seasons is doing well," Rhett said, bringing her gaze back to him. "Hopefully you'll pick up a few tips here that will help with the business."

"How's your job going?" she asked, for want of something else to say.

"Good. I'm working for several major charities, helping their corporate fundraisers with marketing and advertising."

They were so polite, like strangers; cool as stars in the night sky. If someone were watching them, she thought, they would never be able to tell that once they'd blazed like comets, in and out of bed. Her heart still bore the scars from their last, terrible argument. How could he be so calm when her emotions were raging?

"So you're here to pick up tips too?" she asked.

He gave a little sexy smile she remembered so well. She found her lips curving in response.

"Not quite," he said. "I'm the keynote speaker."

Her smile faded. "But..." She lifted the course brochure the organizer had given her as she'd walked in and flipped it open. There was his name, bold as brass, at the top. "I thought Michael Eddings was doing that." She'd been looking forward to listening to the guy who'd been instrumental in marketing a famous brand of Kiwi soft drink.

"He cancelled back in April and they asked me. You should have been notified."

It had probably been mentioned it in one of the many emails she'd received about the course and not read. That would teach her.

"You're the keynote," she clarified.

"Yeah. Watch and learn, baby." He grinned.

Age-old resentment boiled in her stomach. Not only had he intruded on her course, he was the fucking keynote speaker! What a slap in the face. She would have to sit in the audience acting as if he had something to teach her. Yet again, she'd come in second place.

Fighting against the wave of anger that washed over her, she looked out at the foyer again. She couldn't do this. She was too tired, too emotional. It might have been five years since they'd broken up, and he appeared to have gotten over her, but for her it felt like yesterday. She'd come here to try to move on. The absolute worst thing that could have happened was for Rhett to turn up. As much as she hated it, she wasn't over him—she'd never be over him, and if she stayed, she'd just be miserable all week. More miserable. What a waste of time, money, and effort.

"Neve..." He spoke softly, tipping his head to catch her eye. "Don't go."

She looked up at him, her chest heaving. "What makes you think I was leaving? You don't know me, Rhett, not anymore. Don't act as if you can read my mind."

To her surprise, he lifted a hand and placed it on her upper arm. "It's been a long time. I know things ended badly, but a lot of water has passed under the bridge since then. We used to be friends. Wouldn't it be nice to be friends again? Please stay."

Part of her wanted to tear her arm away from his and flounce out of the restaurant like a prima donna, chin in the air. Six months ago, she would have done just that, certain that the world owed her more than a broken heart and a life of loneliness.

But several things had happened since Christmas, including the incident with her father. One of her best friends, Callie, had married in December, and had shortly afterward revealed she was pregnant. Another of her friends, Rowan, had gotten engaged back in April. Then the third member of the Four Seasons, Bridget—or Birdie, as they called her—had announced that her boyfriend, Mal, who'd shied away from commitment for years, had finally proposed, and they were getting married in October. They were all growing up and settling down. Neve was twenty-seven now, nearly twenty-eight, no longer fresh out of university, too old to be going out every night and sleeping around as if she didn't have a care in the world. Somewhere along the way, something had gone very wrong. She was lonely and unhappy, and even though she'd only dated Rhett for a year, and they'd been apart a long time, she missed him—missed the touch of someone who loved her, and missed his friendship.

So, surprising herself, she didn't pull away or snap at him. Instead, she whispered, "Okay."

His eyebrows rose, so he'd obviously not expected his ploy to work, but he smothered his shock with a smile and said, "Want to share a table for breakfast?"

Neve glanced out of the hotel window. When she'd arrived the night before, she'd been stunned at the drop in temperature, having been certain it wouldn't be much different from windy Wellington. While June 21 was the shortest day, it didn't necessarily mark the worst point of winter, which tended to fall later in July. However, she discovered on arrival in Queenstown that the ski season here ran from June 9, and the mountain slopes were already white. They'd had a dusting of snow across the town overnight, and it was freezing outside. To be fair, though, her hotel room had been warm and cozy, and the restaurant had a real fire at one end, so it was hardly cold inside.

Maybe if she continued to think about this trip as an escape, a time out of time, she'd be able to cope. It didn't mean she had to forgive or forget anything that had happened in the past. She would just be putting all the negative feelings, all the hurt and anger and resentment, to one side for a few days, and concentrating on what had been good between them. Because it had been good. She could never argue against that, no matter how much she wished she could.

Chapter Two

To Rhett's complete and utter shock, Neve didn't slap him, yell at him, or stomp off in a huff at his suggestion that they sit and have breakfast together.

Instead, she just said, "Sure," and gave him a wry little smile.

He was so used to her rejecting him that she could have knocked him down with a teeny-tiny feather, but he hid his surprise, gestured toward a table, and followed her over. They took a seat opposite each other, and he smiled up at the waitress as she approached.

"Full English breakfast, please," he said. "With orange juice and a latte."

Neve blew out a breath. "I'll have the same please, but I'll have a long black."

The waitress nodded and went off to relay their order.

"Still got a healthy appetite, I see," Neve said.

He leaned back in his chair and studied her, trying to work out whether her words held a double meaning. Five years ago, he would have been certain they did. It had been a long time, though, since he'd been sure of anything where Neve was concerned.

He'd met her at his best mate's wedding. She'd been twenty-one then and a bridesmaid, along with her three best friends. They'd been dressed as the four seasons, and they'd eventually gone on to use that name for their lingerie business. Neve had been winter, and she'd looked fabulous in a light blue dress that had complemented her stunning, ice-blue eyes that could slice through a man with a simple glance.

At the time, when he'd asked around about the sexy bridesmaid who'd complained loudly about being made to wear a girly gown, Liam—the groom—had told him to approach her with caution. "She scares me shitless," had been Liam's exact words.

Rhett had never seen that side of her though, not until they'd broken up, anyway. In that first year, he would have associated her more with the element of fire than ice. Like most young guys, he'd had a healthy libido, and only food and sport had come close to his love of sex. Previous girlfriends had soon become exasperated with his demands, but Neve had matched him both in and out of the bedroom. They'd had a volatile, tempestuous relationship he'd adored. He'd never minded arguing with her because the making up had been such fun.

And then things had gone terribly, terribly wrong, and he'd finally understood what others had said when they'd called her an ice queen. Standing out naked in the snow wouldn't have been half as cold as being subjected to Neve's glacial fury. He'd loved her, and he'd lost her, and although at the time he'd been angry and determined to forget her, to the end of his days he knew she'd be the love of his life.

He'd changed, though. The traumatic events he'd experienced had made sure of that. Had Neve changed too? On the surface, she hadn't. Of average height, she still had the hourglass figure that had driven him crazy all those years ago—generous bust, generous hips, tiny waist. He'd listened to her talking to the others occasionally, and she was still as opinionated, full of crazy ideas, with bags of confidence, a sharp wit, and a joie de vivre he missed so much it hurt.

At the time, Liam had told him over the phone that she'd reacted to his leaving by going off the rails. Deciding exactly what that meant had kept Rhett awake night after night in strange hotel rooms as he'd traveled around the world. When he'd eventually returned to Wellington, he'd hoped to find she'd outgrown that phase, but it certainly hadn't seemed that way as she'd dated guy after guy as if determined to prove she no longer needed him.

But something had happened over the last six months since Callie and Gene's wedding. She'd lost weight, which was saying something because she'd always exercised and had never been fat. Although still the most beautiful woman he'd ever met, she'd developed dark smudges beneath her eyes. And she carried with her a sense of sadness that hadn't been there before.

Her lips curved up now, though, telling him she had meant the double entendre when she'd enquired if he still had a healthy appetite.

"Always," he said, and winked at her.

She gave a short laugh, her eyes holding a touch of their old sparkle.

He felt a huge wave of relief that she was finally talking to him. He'd seen her name on the list of attendees and had been convinced that when she discovered he was a speaker, she'd turn around and walk straight out.

He decided that staying away from personal chit-chat made sense to start with. "So you're hoping to pick up a few pointers for the business while you're here?"

"Yeah. I want to discover how to use social media to advertise. I want to learn more about how to market our brand on Facebook and Twitter and Instagram. I think we could do well there if I could get my head around it."

"There's definitely a knack to advertising on those channels. Hopefully you'll come out of the course with a bit of know-how to start you off."

She leaned back as the waitress arrived to place their coffees in front of them, then started to sip hers without adding any sugar. No change there then, he thought as he added a spoonful to his latte and stirred it.

"You've done well for yourself," she said. "Landing keynote speaker at a large convention like this is pretty impressive." There didn't seem to be any animosity behind her statement. When he'd first told her his reason for being there, he thought he'd seen anger and jealousy flash across her face, but either he'd been wrong or she was keeping it under control now.

"I would never have said public speaking was my natural forte," he admitted. "But one of the charities I worked for requested I do a seminar for their fundraisers, and it sort of went from there."

"It's funny to see you in a suit. You look all grown up. That year we dated, you were either in your badminton kit or naked whenever I saw you." She sipped her coffee, her eyes gleaming.

He gave a wry smile, deciding not to pursue her down that route just yet. "You look good, too." She wore a smart gray pantsuit and a purple blouse, with a pair of sexy black high heels.

He sipped his coffee, watching her rearrange her cutlery. She didn't know what to make of his compliment. Being with him unnerved her, but she was trying to act like it didn't. He felt an odd sense of relief that she was still affected by his presence, because God knew he was still affected by hers. It had been so long since they'd talked like this. He'd tried to move on over the years, but his feelings for her had not become extinct but had merely lain dormant like a volcano. In spite of everything that had happened between them, he still felt drawn to her.

He'd have to be careful not to go too close to the fire again though. Treat me badly once, shame on you. Treat me badly twice… He sighed as the saying entered his head. It implied that what had gone wrong was all her fault, and that was far from the truth. He placed his coffee cup in the saucer, the shame he'd had to live with for a long time making him sad. Their relationship was like a vase that had not only been broken, it had been smashed into smithereens. There was no hope of being able to glue all the pieces together again and make anything resembling the original article.

He wasn't going to let it get him down, though. It was a glorious, crisp, cold day outside, but in the restaurant it was warm and filled with gorgeous cooking smells. Neve was talking to him, and that gave him a glow that warmed him through.

The waitress approached with their breakfasts and placed them on the table. Rhett tucked into his with gusto, starving as usual. Neve picked at hers. She didn't seem to have much of an appetite, even though she'd ordered the large meal.

"You look tired," he said before thinking that she might take offence at him making a personal observation like that.

She just shrugged and pushed a mushroom around her plate with a fork. "I have insomnia. I don't sleep well."

There were lots of causes of insomnia, but he knew it was linked to depression and anxiety in a major way. Was Neve depressed? Liam had told him she was still single. She lived on her own now Rowan had moved in with her partner, Hitch. Her friends were starting to have stable relationships and settle down. Was that having an effect on her? Or was it something else?

"I saw your advert for the Four Seasons in Women's Weekly," he said. "That was impressive."

She ate a small mouthful of bacon and smirked at him. "Reading ladies' magazines in your spare time now, are we?"

"Absolutely. I need to know what color tights to wear with what boots."

She laughed, and he was pleased to see her shoulders release some of the tension they'd been holding.

"Rhett..." She dipped a piece of sausage into her poached egg. "I was so sorry to hear about your Dad. I should have said that before now."

He paused for a moment, then cut up a hash brown. "Thanks. We got your flowers."

"He was a lovely man. I wish I could have gone to the funeral but... well... it being in Auckland made it difficult... and... it didn't seem right. I didn't think you'd want me there. I didn't want to complicate what must have been an awful day for you."

"You wouldn't have complicated it," he said softly. "I'd love to have seen you. But I understand why you didn't come."

She dropped her gaze to her food and pushed another mushroom around the plate. "How's your mum?"

His mother had suffered terribly, but he didn't want to go into detail. "She's okay now. Trying to rebuild a life alone, which is never easy."

"And Ginny?" She referred to his sister. "How's she doing?"

"She's good. She's dating a guy called Pete. Doing well. He's great with the kids. She seems happy." Ginny's husband had left her and her three children a while ago, and it was a relief to see her happy again.

"Good. I often wondered—did you give up the badminton because of what happened to your dad?"

He leaned back and sipped his coffee. "That played a big part, yeah."

When he'd first met Neve, he'd been surprised and thrilled to discover she shared his love for badminton. He'd played since he was a kid, and he'd been a member of the Under 17 and Under 19 Badminton New Zealand squads back when they were known amusingly as the Black Cocks, a name the organization had since dropped. She'd also been a part of the Women's Under 19 squad, and he'd soon discovered how good she was when they started playing doubles.

They'd made a great team, and they'd trained together for a year. Neve had concentrated mainly on doubles with him, but Rhett had continued his singles training and games and had gone on to win the New Zealand Under 23 National Championship.

Then one of the coaches at the club had told him he wanted him on the squad for the Commonwealth Games in Delhi—on one proviso, that he drop the doubles and concentrate on his singles playing. The coach had pointed out that the two styles of play involved different techniques, and he'd stated quite unambiguously that Neve wasn't good enough to play doubles at international level. Basically, he'd said, she was holding Rhett back, and if he wanted to continue to excel in the game and play at the highest levels, he needed to choose which one to concentrate on.

Highly ambitious, and desperate to play at the highest level, Rhett had chosen singles, and he'd accepted the place on the Commonwealth Games squad on the spot, presuming Neve would be excited for him and would understand why he'd made that choice.

She hadn't. She'd seen his decision as a betrayal—she'd insisted it was not necessarily because he hadn't chosen to play doubles with her, but that he hadn't consulted her before making the decision. They'd argued bitterly about it. At the time, barely twenty-three and with his whole life ahead of him, he'd not understood her anger or why she'd seemed so hurt. He'd been furious that she couldn't be pleased for him or see what a huge opportunity it was. He'd taken her fury for jealousy that he'd been chosen and she hadn't.

Although envy had probably played a small role, as the years had gone by and he'd become older and wiser he'd eventually realized why she'd been so upset. She'd loved him, and they'd been a couple, and taking a place on the squad meant lots of traveling. It would have meant either leaving her behind for months on end or, if she'd chosen to go with him, forcing her to leave her friends and family, as well as the new business she'd just set up with the girls. He should have discussed any decision that had involved their relationship with her first. He'd been selfish, and he'd hurt her.

He felt a wave of sadness, as he always did when he thought of what might have been. At the time, he'd been determined not to regret his decision, and in those first few years he'd worked himself into the ground to prove he'd done the right thing. He'd won a silver medal in the Commonwealth Games and had started training for the Olympics, winning several other smaller tournaments along the way. He'd dated lots of different girls, convinced that what he felt for Neve could be replicated with someone else. And then his father had died.

That in itself probably wouldn't have finished his career, but it had only been the first of a sorry chain of events that had brought things tumbling around his ears. Once he'd known he wouldn't be returning to the game—not at international level, anyway—it had been impossible not to wonder whether he'd done the right thing. He'd lost everything he'd held dear—his father, his career, and Neve, and no matter how much he tried, he knew he'd never be able to get any of them back.

Chapter Three

Rhett had gone quiet, and he looked so sad that Neve felt a strange twist inside.

Was he thinking about his father? Or had her mention of badminton stirred up the same feelings of frustration and melancholy that it did in her?

She set her jaw and refused to feel sorry for him. He'd made his bed, and he had to lie in it. If he was regretting the choices he'd made, so much the better. He'd ruined her life, and he deserved to suffer for what he'd done.

Then he raised his eyes to hers, and Neve caught her breath. She'd forgotten the way just looking into them made her heart race. He held her gaze for a long moment, and she half expected him to say something about his absence, and how he'd missed her. Maybe even to do the one thing he'd never done—apologize.

He didn't, though. Instead, he dropped his gaze to where her hand rested on the table. "No ring," he said. "I thought you'd have been married with six kids by now."

"Six kids in five years?" Smothering frustration that he'd chosen to avoid the opportunity to say he was sorry, she leaned back. "That'd take some doing."

He chuckled. "Yeah, I guess. You're not going steady with anyone, though."

It sounded more like a statement than a question. She guessed he'd asked one of their friends whether she was dating. "Not at the moment. What about you?" She pushed away her plate, unable to eat any more, and sipped her coffee instead. She knew there was no Mrs. Taylor, but she wasn't sure if he was living with anyone, and she would have died rather than ask Liam. "Any girl managed to pin you down?"

"Nope." He didn't elaborate, just smiled.

There must have been other girls, of course, and she was surprised not one had snagged him. He was a good looking guy, funny, warm.

Okay, he could be arrogant and infuriating, but he was great in bed. She could imagine that if he'd met someone less abrasive than herself, who didn't rub him up the wrong way, he'd be a right catch. Why hadn't he found someone else?

When she'd asked him if his father's death had been the reason he'd given up his badminton career, he'd said *That played a big part*. His words implied there was more to it than that, though. He'd loved his badminton—for Christ's sake, he'd even left her for it. What could have made him give it up?

She opened her mouth to ask, but at that moment a woman approached their table.

"Excuse me for interrupting." She bent to smile at Rhett. "I wonder if I could borrow you for a while—we need to set up your laptop and connect it to the projector."

"Sure." Rhett put his serviette on the table and gave Neve an apologetic smile. "Sorry."

"It's okay, go on."

He stood and paused. "Can we catch up later?"

It had unsettled her to talk to him, and she wasn't sure she wanted to make a habit of it. But the woman was waiting and it seemed rude to say no, so she just nodded, and he moved away.

Neve gestured to the waitress and asked for another coffee, hoping to quell the butterflies that continued to flutter in her stomach. She stared out of the window, breathing deeply, trying to calm herself. The hotel overlooked Lake Wakatipu and the snow-topped mountain range known as the Remarkables. It was the perfect setting for a winter adventure. She'd hoped this course might mark a turning point for her. She could never have guessed this twist of events, though.

Her coffee arrived, and she sipped it slowly. Her stomach began to settle. How strange that he could still have such an effect on her, even after all these years.

It had only affected her because he'd been out of context. She hadn't expected to see him here, and it had taken her by surprise, that was all.

Even as she told herself that, she knew she was fooling herself. She still got that flip in her stomach, that missing heartbeat, every time she saw him, even if she knew he was going to join her group of friends for a drink.

As always, sadness mixed with anger that he had this power over her. Twelve months wasn't an immense length of time to be in a relationship with someone, for heaven's sake. It was a drop in the ocean compared to her parents, who'd just celebrated their thirtieth wedding anniversary.

But how you feel about someone has no correlation to the amount of time you've been with them. Her relationship with Rhett had consisted of an electrifying intensity. People had remarked upon it at the time, commenting on how they were so in love, so crazy about one another. They'd crammed a lifetime of loving into one year, and she'd not just liked him, not even just loved him. She'd been absolutely besotted with him, and he—or so she'd thought at the time—with her. They'd been inseparable, and their love of badminton had only served to bring them closer together. Again, or so she'd thought.

Nowadays, she tended to steer her mind away from musing on their breakup, but for the first time in ages she let herself remember that fateful night. Rhett had usually done the cooking in their house, but that day he'd been away at a match in Auckland, and so she'd baked lasagna ready for him when he walked in, around seven p.m.

They'd sat down to eat, but even before she'd put a fork into her pasta, she'd known something was bothering him. Strangely quiet, he'd been unable to meet her eyes. Heart racing, she'd asked what was wrong, and then he'd told her that the coach wanted him on the squad for the Commonwealth Games—as a singles player.

She would readily admit that her first emotions had been jealousy and resentment. She was a damn good badminton player, and they'd been a damn good doubles team. She'd known he was better than her, although she would never have admitted it to his face, but in spite of that, she'd read him well on the court, and they'd won lots of tournaments together. By choosing singles, he'd relegated her sporting career to the dustbin, because she'd known she wasn't good enough to make it on her own.

Whatever faults she'd had, though, she hadn't thought of herself as a small person, and she would have been happy for him eventually. She would have continued to train with him and push him, and would happily have traveled with him all over the world.

But before she'd said anything, he'd lifted his chin, looked her in the eye, and told her he'd made his decision, and he'd chosen to go.

He couldn't have hurt her more if he'd slapped her hard around the face. If the roles had been reversed, she would never have made a decision that would have affected them both without discussing it with him first. But what had made her really angry had been the defiant glint in his eye. He'd expected her to object, and to fight him about it.

She knew that arguments weren't necessarily a terrible thing in a relationship. Standing up to one another stopped a person taking the other for granted. Coming from an extremely strict upbringing, she'd been determined that her partner would not railroad her into decisions or walk all over her, and it excited her to stand up to Rhett and to be able to lay out her point of view. She'd known it turned him on, too, having her fight with him, because after thirty minutes of yelling at each other he'd always pulled her into his arms and smothered her protests with kisses until eventually she'd gone limp and let him make love to her. He'd always been physical in their lovemaking, enjoying dominating her in the bedroom because it was the only place she'd let him, and even though part of her hated that he could end an argument that way, it had turned her on too, so she'd always let him.

But that day, she'd refused to give in. The betrayal had been too big, too deep, to be smoothed over with his attempt to end it with sex. He'd tried to manhandle her into the bedroom. She'd fought him, screaming, crying with frustration, and eventually he'd realized it wasn't all part of the usual making up process and she was genuinely furious and upset with him.

They'd stayed up all night, fighting, crying, talking, and fighting again. She'd tried to explain why he'd upset her, but he'd refused to apologize, saying it was sour grapes and that her resentment stemmed from jealousy because he'd been chosen over her. He'd been angry that she couldn't be pleased for him. They'd yelled, banged doors—she'd even thrown the whole dish of lasagna at him.

For the first night since they'd gotten together, he'd slept on the sofa.

All through the next week, the atmosphere had been icy, both of them refusing to give any ground.

That weekend, she'd finally moved out.

She sat back in her seat, misery settling over her like the low clouds that clustered over the tops of the Remarkables. Rhett had left the country not long after, and he hadn't tried to contact her for several years. She'd only received news about him through the badminton club or through Liam, with whom he'd remained in touch from time to time. It was through Liam that she'd heard about Rhett's father, and part of the reason why she hadn't gone to the funeral was because Rhett hadn't rung her to tell her he'd passed away. She'd been convinced he'd wanted nothing to do with her.

That seemed to have changed, though. In fact, he seemed to have changed. While they'd dated, he'd been constantly on the move—when he wasn't playing badminton, he'd run miles every day and trained in things like martial arts and parkour to improve his flexibility. His personality had reflected his physical side—he'd been enthusiastic and impulsive, with a hot temper that had flared in seconds and disappeared just as quickly. When he'd returned to Wellington, however, he'd seemed different—calmer, less angry, more laid back. He'd finally tried to talk to her, but by then the years of feeling neglected and being cold-shouldered had built a barrier of ice around her, and she'd wanted nothing to do with him.

She still wanted nothing to do with him. She finished off her coffee. Okay, she could accept that it wouldn't be the worst thing in the world if they were on talking terms. It made her friends uncomfortable when the two of them were in close proximity, and she knew they'd like to have him around more. If she could have a decent conversation with him, be polite, and be civil, then that was a good thing. Maybe they'd both grown up and finally moved on.

She looked out, watching tiny snowflakes whip across the street in the brisk, wintry wind. She hadn't moved on. That was her problem. He'd traveled and continued with his career, and even though he'd eventually returned, he'd obviously changed and had been able to put the past behind him. Neve didn't know how to do that. When she'd been with him, it was as if she'd opened her ribcage and exposed her heart to him, and he'd wrenched it out of her chest and stomped on it. How could a person ever recover from that?

Slowly, she got to her feet and walked out of the restaurant. She'd come here to try to make a new start. Rhett's appearance might, at first glance, seem like a spoke in the wheel, but maybe it was a good thing. Seeing him over the next few days would reinforce how she needed to get over her issues and move on with her life.

Returning to her room, she collected her laptop, notebook, pens, and anything else she thought she might need for the morning's session, and then returned to the main conference room ten minutes before nine. Rhett was already there, at the front, talking to a couple of the organizers. Neve ignored him and took a seat at a table near the back. Three men and one woman were already seated there, and they exchanged introductions and got themselves coffee before one of the organizers took the podium to announce they were ready to start.

The room fell quiet, apart from the shuffling of papers and the scrape of chairs as those coming in late found a place and everyone made themselves comfortable. Neve left her laptop shut. Regardless of her personal feelings for Rhett, his aim as keynote speaker was to establish the framework for the convention and summarize the core message of the events rather than go into detail at this stage about techniques or strategies, so she wasn't expecting to take heaps of notes.

Although she wouldn't necessarily have labeled one of his skills as public speaking, in another way she wasn't surprised he'd discovered he was good at it. He had a natural charm, an easygoing manner, and he was warm and funny. It would be interesting to hear how he came across to a large crowd such as this one.

The conference organizer began by giving a general introduction, welcoming everyone, laying out a brief summary of the plan of events, and going through basic details such as times of breaks and where the fire exits were.

"Now we've got all that out of the way," she said, "it's time for me to introduce to you our keynote speaker. With an A+ Bachelor of Commerce degree from Victoria University in Wellington and several years in marketing working with charities to improve their corporate fundraising, you'd expect a twenty-eight-year-old's CV to end there. However, our speaker has also won a silver medal in Badminton singles at the Commonwealth Games, which suggests his talents are many and varied."

Was it Neve's imagination, or did the young organizer's lips quirk up as she cast a glance at Rhett? He was looking at his feet, however, and missed the flirtatious look, if it was one.

"So without further ado, will you please welcome Rhett Taylor."

Everyone clapped as he walked to the podium. Next to her, the other woman at the table, whose name Neve had discovered was Carol, leaned toward her and whispered, "I've heard this guy is very good."

"Mmm," Neve said non-committedly.

"And he's hot," Carol murmured.

Neve gave a short laugh. Yeah, she couldn't deny that. He'd always looked good in casual clothes, in his white badminton gear or his tight jeans, but in his navy suit he looked stylish and sophisticated. Wow, he really had changed.

She settled back in her chair, interested now to hear what he had to say. Would he just talk business? Or would he give any insight into the end of his sporting career, and whatever had happened to bring him back to Wellington?

Chapter Four

Rhett stood next to the podium, which was raised on a small stage so everyone in the audience could see who was speaking. Behind his back he held a remote control, so he was able to change the slide on his PowerPoint without walking over to his laptop each time. He did it now, glancing up at the screen behind him and watching as the name of the conference faded to his own name, complete with his job title and qualifications.

He had a small microphone clipped to his lapel, so his voice came across loud and clear.

"Good morning, everyone." He walked a little to the right side of the stage so he didn't block the screen. "My name's Rhett Taylor, although I fully expect at least six of you to call me Rhett Butler by the end of the conference." He smiled, and everyone laughed. It wasn't a joke. He'd lay money on someone getting his name wrong before lunch, let alone the end of the course.

It wasn't the first time he'd spoken in public, but it was the largest conference he'd been to, and he had to admit to feeling a little daunted as he looked across the sea of faces. Neve sat at the back, leaning on the table, her chin on her hand as she watched him. He hadn't expected her to be in the audience when he'd written the first draft of his keynote speech, before he'd seen the list of attendees. Even when he'd seen her name, he'd expected her to walk out when she realized he was the keynote. But she hadn't—she'd stayed, and now part of his mind argued furiously with itself about whether he should change one of the main elements he'd planned to mention. Removing it from the speech would make it shorter and would mean things wouldn't link together as well. But keeping it in would mean finally revealing to Neve what he'd tried to keep secret from her for the last two years. What should he do?

"We're all here to learn more about marketing, promotion, and advertising." He changed the screen to show a bullet-pointed list. "Specifically, we all want to know how we can improve our sales utilizing things like social media, including Facebook, Twitter, LinkedIn, Instagram, Pinterest, Google Plus, and Tumblr, all of which have over a hundred million users across the world. We'll also be looking at some others that maybe you're not so familiar with, such as VK, Flickr, Vine, Meetup, Tagged, and Ask.fm, which all have over thirty-seven million users. And why limit ourselves to English-speaking customers? We'll touch on sites like Ibibo, India's largest online travel company, and Meilishuo, a Chinese community website that specializes in women's fashion, which has over a hundred-and-fifty million users."

He glanced to the back of the room. He'd put that in there for her. Had her lips curved up? He wasn't sure—her hand partly covered her face.

He turned away and began to walk slowly across the stage, knowing he had to make a decision now on whether to stick to his original speech. He gave a little sigh. Ultimately, what was the point in keeping it a secret any longer? He'd keep the speech as it was, and *que sera, sera*. What will be, will be.

"I'm going to start by telling you a little about myself," he began. "I won't drone on for long because this isn't about me, but events over the past few years have directly affected where I've ended up, and I hope that by sharing the things I've discovered along the way I might be able to help others."

He paused to sip from a cup of water, then carried on. "As Lisa just mentioned, three years ago I was at the height of my sporting career. I'd won a silver medal at the Commonwealth Games, and first place in seven other major international tournaments. I was at the peak of my fitness, and was poised ready to take over the world." He smiled, and a few people chuckled.

"Then came the first bombshell," he continued. "My father discovered he had testicular cancer. Unbeknown to his family, he'd had it for years but hadn't wanted to see a doctor, and because of that it was extremely advanced. He died within two months of being diagnosed."

Neve was looking down at her notepad—was she writing or doodling while she thought about his words? She'd liked his dad, and his dad had thought she was wonderful. A lump grew in his throat.

Kia kaha, Rhett. He could almost hear his dad saying the Maori words. *Stay strong.*

"That in itself shook my world," he said. "I came home to help my mother through that difficult time, and ended up staying for a few months to sort through his effects and to work out her finances. It was only supposed to be a brief respite, though—I had my next tournament lined up, and I was still training."

He took a deep breath. "And then came the second bombshell. Just six months after my father was diagnosed with testicular cancer, so was I."

Neve's head snapped up. Her eyes widened, and even though her hand covered her mouth, he could see her jaw sagging.

Part of him regretted saying anything now—he hadn't wanted her to know. He wasn't sure why. They'd said some terribly cruel things to each other in the past, but he couldn't imagine she'd be anything but horrified to hear the truth. Maybe he didn't want her to be nice to him just because he'd had cancer. Or maybe he just didn't want to upset her. Whatever, it was done now.

"Don't worry," he said wryly to the audience, the majority of whose faces showed pity and shock that the young, apparently fit guy before them had been ill, "this isn't going to be all doom and gloom, so you can put away your tissues." A few people smiled, but he could see he'd touched them all, because everyone knew someone who'd had cancer.

"My father's cancer had spread beyond his lymph nodes to his lungs, liver, and bones," he continued. "But luckily I'd caught mine early. I had an operation and some radiotherapy, and although I'll need to have regular checkups, I've been given the all clear."

He glanced over at Neve again. She still had her hand over her mouth, and he could see the woman next to her leaning forward and whispering something. Neve shook her head, and the woman rubbed her back.

He'd upset her, and briefly he felt a twinge of guilt that she'd found out like this. He should have told her first. *Fuck*. What was her reaction going to be? Would she be angry with him?

"It's great news," he carried on, because he couldn't do anything else. "But that's not the point. The point is that men whose fathers have had testicular cancer are around four times more likely to develop it. I didn't know that, and neither did my father, as far as I know. You see, my grandfather also died from it. If I'd known about the increased risk, I would have pushed my father to get tested. But I didn't. Because cancer's frightening, and most people would rather not know if they have a problem, which is crazy because the earlier you are diagnosed, the better your chance of recovery. But I do understand that talking about your crown jewels is embarrassing, let alone unzipping your fly to the family doctor."

A few men laughed, obviously having had firsthand experience with that.

"The death of my father, and my own illness, are the two life-changing events that made me decide to give up my badminton career and focus instead on something that could help others." With the worst part out of the way, he'd warmed up now, and could start getting into the meat of what everyone had come there to learn. But he'd made that human connection, and he could see that nobody in the room remained untouched by his words.

"I decided that I wanted to work with charities to help them raise money, and also to teach people who worked with them better ways to connect with people about this disease, in the hope not only of taking away any fear connected with it, but also of improving communication so that more people will become aware of methods of self-examination, and what to do if they discover something worrying."

He sipped from his cup of water again. "When I started connecting with charities, it surprised me how many of them were unclear about social networking and the ways it can be utilized to spread the word. And this is the key—I realized that it's not about listing facts, yelling in people's faces, and demanding money all the time. Nobody wants to read about their chances of contracting cancer or to see requests for donations in their Facebook feed, and it's the same with your businesses—constant in-your-face demands to buy this or that will quickly be passed over. Well-thought-out advertising involves making a connection with people that means they can't help but click on that advert because it includes something directly relevant to themselves. And that's what we're here to learn about today."

He clicked the remote and brought up the course's agenda. "We're going to break this down into four separate areas. The first day we'll look at the difference between marketing, promotion, and advertising. Yes, there is a difference." He grinned at the audience, and everyone laughed. "Then we'll look in more detail at the different types of social networking sites and which would be the best for your business. Next we'll examine in detail ways of advertising on these sites and give you some insider tips, and then finally we'll work in groups so you can discuss methods with people who run businesses similar to yours, and hopefully exchange some ideas. Plus there's the planned visit tomorrow afternoon to Sky Peak to study the ski industry and—more importantly—the distillery, purely for research purposes of course."

Smiling and glancing to the back of the room, he stopped with some surprise because Neve had vanished. There wasn't much he could do about it, though, because he hadn't finished his speech yet.

So he carried on, trying to concentrate, going into a bit more detail about what knowledge the attendees could hope to gain by the end of the course, and relating a few facts and figures about return on investment and the kind of difference the right advertising could make to sales, giving examples of his own successes to illustrate.

He finished just before ten o'clock and left the stage to a round of applause. He sat to one side, relieved he'd finished, the response from the audience positive enough to convince him he'd done okay.

Lisa, the conference organizer, retook the podium and spoke in a bit more detail about what they could expect. She was an attractive woman, about his own age, slim and with long blonde hair, and she reacted to him in a way that told him she found him attractive, touching his arm when she spoke to him, leaning toward him, and meeting his gaze with a look in her eye that suggested she'd be interested in getting to know him better.

A few years ago, he might have thought about asking her to join him for a drink later. After breaking up with Neve, as he traveled from tournament to tournament around the world, he'd done his best to put her behind him, determined that replacing her would be an easy task, and there were plenty more fish in the Pacific, Atlantic, and Indian Oceans.

None of them had ever touched his heart the way Neve had, though. The longest time he'd stayed with a girl had been six months in Australia leading up to the Oceania Championships. Sarah had been quiet, gentle, and pretty, and they'd spent a lot of time together, but even though he still kept in touch with her, he'd not wanted to continue their relationship enough to move to Australia, or to ask her to move to New Zealand with him.

Neve had returned toward the end of his speech, taking her place at the back again. He glanced across at her. She didn't look at him but sat quietly, studying her notebook, her face pale. He'd never been able to work out exactly what it was about her that fascinated him so much. Maybe it was because she was such a complicated character, full of layers like an onion—no matter how many he'd peeled back, he'd just uncovered even more beneath.

On the surface, she was courageous, feisty, and in-your-face, but beneath that lay a woman more vulnerable than she cared to admit. With a soft spot for animals and children, she'd always been the first person to drop whatever she was doing to help out someone in trouble. He'd loved that about her—that strange dichotomy between her wicked sense of humor and her fierce defense of anyone who needed protecting.

Lisa was rounding up her talk, and at ten thirty it was time for a short break before they got stuck into the first workshops of the day. She came over, thanked him, and tried to get him to join her at a table, but he extricated himself gently, got himself a coffee, and headed toward the back of the room.

He was interrupted several times along the way by people who wanted to thank him for his speech and who were eager to talk about their own experiences.

Each time, he listened briefly, then moved on, but it still took him nearly ten minutes to get to the table at the back.

As he approached, Neve got to her feet. He walked up to her warily, not sure what her reaction was going to be. They were in public, so he hoped she wasn't going to be too angry with him. They didn't have time for a long discussion because it was only supposed to be a fifteen minute break.

She met his gaze as he stopped before her. He put his coffee on the table. "Neve…"

Shaking her head, she held out a hand. Puzzled, he took it, and she closed her cool fingers around his. Then she turned and led the way out of the conference room.

Still unsure what her reaction was going to be, he followed her out, along the corridor, and into the foyer. She walked to one side, leading him behind a pillar so they were out of sight of the front desk.

He looked down at her, not sure what to say, knowing only that he liked the touch of her hand on his, and that he still thought she was the most beautiful woman he'd ever seen.

She met his gaze for a long moment. And then she moved forward, slid her arms around his waist, and rested her cheek on his chest.

Chapter Five

Neve wasn't sure what Rhett's reaction would be. Half of her expected him to grab her by her upper arms, thrust her away, and ask her what the hell she thought she was doing. He did inhale sharply, so it was obvious that she'd taken him by surprise.

But then he lifted his arms and brought them around her, and she felt his lips rest on her hair.

"It's okay." He rubbed her back with one hand. "I'm all right."

She couldn't have put into words the hundreds of conflicting emotions that were knotted like skeins of wool inside her at that moment. She couldn't even untangle them herself, let alone explain them to him.

When he'd first announced the words, *Just six months after my father was diagnosed with testicular cancer, so was I*, for a few moments she'd thought she hadn't heard right. He'd had cancer? Complete bewilderment had made her stare at him as her heart had shuddered to a stop. He'd had *cancer*? And he hadn't told her? Why hadn't he told her? How could something so horrendous, so momentous, have happened to him and she was unaware of it?

It was as if she'd discovered there had been a terrible catastrophe somewhere in the world, like a meteor crashing to Earth and wiping out a whole continent, but she'd been on holiday without the internet and hadn't heard about it until she'd gotten back. How could she not have known this? They'd been so close—she thought she would have felt something like that in her blood.

But she hadn't. A wave of anger and hurt had swept over her at that realization, so strong and fierce it had made her feel faint. And then in a split second it had vanished. Why would he tell her? They weren't in a relationship. She'd made it quite clear she didn't want to hear from him again. Maybe he'd thought she wouldn't be interested. Or maybe he just hadn't wanted to complicate what must have been an awful time for him so soon after losing his own father to exactly the same disease.

He'd had cancer. The realization had finally settled like a feather floating to the ground. He and his family would have coped with it as best as they could.

Oh, his poor, poor mother.

She moved back a little. Tears stung her eyes, but she'd never liked crying in front of people, and she fought to make sure they didn't fall.

"So you're okay now?" she whispered.

She still had her arms around him, and he didn't lower his.

"I'm fine." He dipped his head so he could meet her eyes. "Luckily, I caught it early. It hadn't spread, and I've had the all clear. There's no reason to think it will come back."

She swallowed hard and nodded. "Okay." Out of the corner of her eye, she saw the organizer exit the corridor, obviously looking for him. She moved back reluctantly, and he dropped his arms, also reluctantly, unless she was imagining it.

"She's looking for you." She gestured toward the blonde. "I think she has the hots for you."

His lips curved up. "Lisa's just being nice."

"No she's not. She wants to get in your pants." Even as she joked, she felt a sharp pain inside her at the thought of the operation and the treatment he'd had. Jesus. What effect had it had on him?

He just laughed though, and rolled his eyes. "You know I'm not interested in blondes." He winked at her.

She gave a wry smile and wrapped her arms around herself, shivering a little. "There's no time now. Maybe we can talk more later?"

"Of course." He hesitated, glancing over to where Lisa had approached the front desk, possibly to ask if they'd seen him. "Neve—I am sorry you had to find out like that. I should have told you this morning, if not a lot, lot earlier. I just…" He shrugged.

"Not now," she said, seeing the receptionist point at them and Lisa glance over. "It's okay. Don't worry about it. You've got more important things to concentrate on today than me."

He opened his mouth to reply, but at that moment Lisa rounded the pillar, stopping with surprise at the sight of both them.

"Oh, I'm so sorry." She gave them both a genuine smile. "I didn't mean to interrupt."

"It's okay," Neve said. "We're old friends and we're just catching up. I didn't mean to drag him away. I'll leave you to it." Before either of them could say anything else, she slipped away and walked back to the conference room.

Carol, who was sitting beside her at their table, had obviously seen her with him and gave her a smile as she returned. "Are you okay?"

"Yeah, thanks." Neve took her seat and accepted the coffee the woman had kindly brought her. "He's an old friend. I hadn't realized he'd been ill, that's all."

"What a shock for you. It's a terrible disease, isn't it? My brother-in-law had bowel cancer. Had the op and the treatment though, and he's still going strong fifteen years later."

"Yes, it's amazing what they can do now."

Carol continued to chatter on with positive stories about people recovering from the disease. Neve didn't want to interrupt her when she was obviously trying to offer comfort, but she only half listened, her mind still trying to process everything.

At one point, she felt a hand on her shoulder and glanced up as Rhett leaned across to pick up the coffee he'd left there. He squeezed her shoulder before returning to the front of the room, where he took a seat as the next speaker walked up to the podium to begin her talk.

Neve opened her laptop to prepare to write some notes, and settled down as the woman started speaking. It was an interesting seminar on the difference between some of the social networking sites and which ones were best to target depending on the kind of product being sold, but even though her fingers tapped automatically at the keys, at the end of the session she stared blankly at the words on the screen, hardly remembering typing them.

The rest of the morning passed in much the same way. Neve concentrated as best she could, hoping to catch up with him when they broke at one o'clock, but unfortunately when it came to lunch Lisa whisked him away to sit with some of the other speakers, so she didn't have an opportunity to talk to him.

After catching a quick bite with Carol and some of the others, she excused herself and took a walk outside, hoping to blow away the cobwebs before the afternoon session.

She only had her suit jacket to keep her warm and consequently felt the bite of the wintry wind as she crossed the road to look out across Lake Wakatipu. Snow had continued to fall all morning, but it was fine as talcum powder, melting on contact with her jacket and hair rather than coating it.

Shoving her hands in her pockets, she walked slowly along the Lake Esplanade. Large trees lined a grassy verge that also bore tall lampposts that reminded her of the one in *The Lion, the Witch and the Wardrobe*. The gardens on the peninsula opposite were lined with dark green conifers that formed a fringe around the cool blue lake. It was all very beautiful, but she found it difficult to enjoy it.

"Hey."

With surprise, she turned to see Rhett walking toward her. He'd donned a padded gray jacket that made him look more like his old self, and she had to catch her breath as he crossed the road and approached her.

"It's fucking freezing out here." He stuffed his hands in his pockets. "Are you mad?"

She gave a short laugh. "Just wanted to stretch my legs."

"You should at least have brought a coat."

"Yeah." She shrugged. "Maybe."

"Let's walk a bit. It might stop your joints freezing up."

She fell into step beside him, and they strolled along the path fronting the lake.

"Lisa let you out, then?" she teased.

He grinned. "It wouldn't surprise me to turn around and find her shadowing us." They both glanced over their shoulders, and then laughed.

"I don't blame her," Neve said. "Your speech made you seem quite a catch."

"Apart from the fact that I announced to the whole conference that I've had the crown jewels interfered with?" His smile faded as he looked at her. "Aw, come on. You've got to be able to laugh about it or what's the point?"

"I found out about two hours ago, Rhett. Forgive me if I'm not splitting my sides just yet."

His lips twisted. "Yeah, all right. Fair enough." He tipped his head back and blew out a breath, watching it turn to white mist in front of his face. "Are you mad at me?"

"Yes. No. Kind of."

"Glad we cleared that up."

"Of course I'm mad at you," she said, somewhat heatedly. "Part of me is incredibly hurt that you never told me. I understand why you didn't at the time—we weren't in contact, and after what happened to your dad I can get why you'd want to close ranks with the family and deal with it yourself. It's just... It's odd to think you've been in Wellington for, what, eighteen months? And it's never come up."

"Nobody knows," he said gently.

"Not even Liam?" That shocked her—he'd been best man at Liam's wedding, and the two of them had been mates since school.

"Nope. I haven't told anyone. Only Ginny and my mum. I had the treatment in Auckland while I was staying with her, and I swore them both to secrecy." He hunched his shoulders, shoving his hands deeper in his pockets. "It's hard to explain what it was like. Coming straight out of my dad's passing... When I sat in front of the consultant and he told me, the first person I thought of was my mum and how it was going to destroy her. Telling her was the hardest thing I've ever had to do."

"I can imagine."

"Dealing with the op and the treatment was only part of it. I felt like a wounded animal. I didn't want to see or talk to anyone. I just wanted to crawl into a hole until it had all gone away."

Neve swallowed hard. He was normally such an outgoing person; it gave her a pain in her chest to think of him becoming so introverted.

"I didn't ever make a decision not to tell you," he said. "There were times when all I wanted to do was pick up the phone and hear your voice."

"You should have," she whispered.

"Yeah. Maybe."

They continued walking for a while, not saying anything. The brisk wind poked fingers through the gaps in her clothes, and Neve shivered.

"Here." He unzipped his coat.

"No, no," she protested, but he'd already shrugged it off, and he placed it around her shoulders. She squashed a brief flare of irritation. He'd always been like this—acting like a gentleman, whether she wanted his help or not. But how can you criticize someone who's trying to be nice?

Besides, she was cold. She pulled the coat close around her, enjoying the way it still carried some of his body heat, as well as the faint aroma of his aftershave.

He turned the collar of his suit jacket up and shoved his hands in the pockets of his trousers.

"Do you want to tell me about your treatment?" she asked. "You don't have to if you don't want to, but I'd like to know."

He shrugged. "One thing I learned very quickly is that you can't hold onto your dignity when you have testicular cancer. Well, actually that's unfair. They do everything they can to try to let you keep your dignity. I guess privacy is a better description."

"Deana said it's like that when you have a baby." Neve's sister had given birth to her second only a month ago. "Once the doctor and his team have had their heads down there, you stop worrying about covering yourself up every time someone walks in the room."

He laughed. "Yeah."

"How did you discover you had it?"

"Found a lump. In my right testicle."

She couldn't help it—she had to tease him. "While playing with yourself?"

He glanced at her, a little warily, and for a brief moment she wondered whether he'd been dating someone at the time. Maybe a girl had found it? She was surprised at the stab of jealousy she felt at the thought of him being intimate with someone else. She'd trained herself not to think about it, and it almost took her breath away.

But his lips had quirked up. "No. Just a monthly self-exam, the same way women are supposed to check their breasts."

"Yeah, right."

He grinned. "Anyway, went to the doctor, who sent me for scans. It all happened pretty quickly. I had an op, and then because my dad and grandad had also had cancer, they gave me radiotherapy to the lymph nodes to make sure it wasn't going to spread. Didn't have to have chemo, thank God. In six months, it was all done."

She nodded. "And you feel well now?"

"I feel great. I have to have regular checkups, and… you know… keep an eye on the area, that's all."

She was so relieved that it made her want to tease him. "If you need help with your self-exam, just say."

That made him chuckle. "I'll bear it in mind."

"I can even check your prostate, if you want."

He stopped walking. Surprised, she stopped too and turned to face him, expecting him to scold her.

"I can still get a hard-on," he said mildly, "so it might be best to limit talk like that when I have to return to the conference in five minutes."

She bit her lip but couldn't stop the laughter bubbling up, and eventually he joined in.

"Sorry," she said when she eventually got control of herself.

"I'd much rather you tease me than be angry with me." His gaze caressed her, suddenly sultry, causing her heart to hammer.

She wasn't sure what to say to that. She felt all mixed up and confused. It was like she'd spent five years convinced the world had stopped turning and she would have to live the rest of her life in eternal night, and then suddenly the birds had started singing, heralding the coming of dawn.

She turned and began walking back to the hotel, and he fell into step beside her. She buried her chin in the collar of his jacket, conscious of him next to her, his arm only an inch from hers. She could feel herself thawing, warming through every time he smiled. But this didn't mean anything, and she had to make sure she kept her distance. He'd always had this effect on her, this ability to cloud her judgment, and to stir her up until all she could think about was pulling him close and lifting her lips to his for a kiss. That would be a terrible idea. Either he'd push her away and ask her what the hell she was playing at, or he'd kiss her back, and that would never end well. He'd hurt her too much in the past for her to ever get over it.

But she'd missed him so much, and it was nice to be with him, and to talk and laugh a little, if nothing else.

Chapter Six

The afternoon passed relatively quickly for Rhett. He wasn't sure if Neve felt the same warmth in her stomach that he felt in his after their talk at lunch, but every time he glanced over she was smiling and talking to the other people at her table, so he suspected she felt better after speaking to him.

He'd hoped to catch up with her again, but a guy who wanted to talk about corporate fundraising caught him at the start of the afternoon interval and kept him talking. There were more workshops until late because everyone wanted to get their money's worth out of the time they were spending there, and to his disappointment at the end of the day when he finished talking to Lisa and the other organizers, Neve had already left the conference hall.

He went up to his room and had just made himself a cup of coffee when his phone rang. The screen read "Hitch". Nathan Hitchcock, or Hitch as everyone—including his fiancée, Rowan—called him, was another good mate, and he'd known that Neve was going to be at the conference. Rhett answered the phone with a wry smile.

"Hello?"

"Hey." The grin in Hitch's voice was evident from the first word. "How did it go? Have you killed each other yet?"

Rhett chuckled and took his coffee cup over to the bed. Sitting back against the pillows, he took a sip before answering. "Clearly not, as I'm talking to you. She was surprisingly mellow. I think she's coming down with something."

Hitch laughed. "Aw. Poor Neve. Was it a shock for her, do you think, seeing you there?"

"You could say that. Her eyes almost fell out of her head and rolled along the floor."

"I bet. Was she angry? I was certain she'd walk straight out once she saw you."

"She wasn't too pleased—you were right. But we got talking, and we actually had breakfast together."

"Fucking hell."

"I know. Wonders will never cease."

"So... where from here?"

"Don't know," Rhett said honestly. "I was going to ask her to join me for dinner but I missed her. I'll try to catch her in the restaurant."

"And after dinner?"

Rhett sipped his coffee. "Don't start."

"I'm just saying... Middle of winter, temperature's dropping, she'll be feeling the cold, looking for someone to warm her up..."

"Hitch, shut up. That's not what this is about. All I wanted was for her to talk to me."

Hitch chuckled. "Yeah, I know. I'm poking a sleeping bear, aren't I? Look, it's great that she didn't kill you on sight. It's a step forward, isn't it?"

"It's come to something when not being murdered is considered a step forward in a relationship."

"I know, but this is you and Neve we're talking about. Hey, I got another commission. Rowan and I are off to South America next week..."

Hitch went on to talk about his latest photography job. Rhett listened, pleased for his friend, but his mind wandered, Hitch's words clinging to him like clear wrap.

She'll be looking for someone to warm her up...

He shook his head. *Nope, nope, nope.* Going down that road was suicide. It was a route full of potholes and speed bumps with fallen trees lying across it. It was a crazy idea to think they'd be able to take the leap from not murdering each other to having sex.

His lips curved up. She'd been fantastic in bed. Feisty enough to make a man's hair stand on end, pliant enough to make him weak at the knees. It was a nice fantasy.

"I'd better go," Hitch said. "Rowan's got some kind of fashion show tonight with Callie, and I promised I'd go for moral support."

"Not because you want to ogle all the chicks in lingerie?"

"I can't believe you'd even suggest that."

Rhett laughed. "See you later."

"Yeah, see ya."

Rhett hung up and tossed the phone onto the bed, finished off his coffee, lay back on the pillows, and closed his eyes.

When he'd left New Zealand, as the years had passed, Neve's face had blurred in his mind, and when he'd tried to remember what she was like, he'd received snapshot sensations rather than images. The silkiness of her dark bob. The smoothness of her skin, especially on the areas she didn't expose to the sun—the curve of her breasts, the inside of her thighs. The smell of the perfume she used to wear that lingered on her clothes and in her hair. The lift he felt in his heart when she laughed, when she kissed him, when he looked into her eyes and saw the desire he felt for her mirrored there.

Now, though, he was able to add images to the feelings. The unusual, icy-blue color of her eyes. Her sexy smile when she teased him. The gorgeous curves of her body in the stylish suit, with the V of her shirt open and exposing her creamy skin...

He opened his eyes and sighed. No, he'd been right the first time. Thinking about her like that was a bad idea. It would be fun, but even if she'd consider it—which she wouldn't—he didn't want to get involved with her. He wasn't sure he was strong enough to survive having his heart broken again.

Checking the time on his phone, he saw it was six-forty-five, with only fifteen minutes until dinner. Members of the conference paid a flat fee to have a three course meal included every evening, with a separate room in the restaurant reserved just for them. Would she be at his table?

He rose and changed out of his suit, tidied himself up and added some aftershave, and put on a more informal jacket and trousers, leaving on the white shirt but removing his tie. With five minutes to go, he left his room and made his way downstairs.

He was relieved to find Neve not yet seated, talking to a guy by the door. He stopped walking, picked up a pamphlet from Reception, and pretended to read it. The man was older than her, probably in his early forties, but fairly good looking. He was definitely interested in her judging by the way he leaned on the doorjamb toward her. He whispered something and she laughed. The guy smiled back, clearly pleased at her reaction.

Rhett's lips curved up. *She's not interested, dude,* he thought. He knew her well enough to know the man was too short, and that his build—on the wrong side of being overweight—his ostentatious, flashy watch, and his shiny suit wouldn't appeal to her. The guy was also sweating quite a bit—a real turn-off, if ever he'd seen one.

Sure enough, she took a step back and glanced around the foyer, and her face lit up as her gaze fell on him. "Excuse me," he heard her say, "I've just seen a friend," and she smiled and crossed the tiled floor toward him.

Replacing the pamphlet on the counter, he watched her approach. She'd changed too, into a more casual pair of gray trousers with a cream shirt, the bottom of which peeked out under a black sweater, but she still wore the sexy black high heels.

Down boy.

"Glad to hear you consider me a friend now," he said.

She rolled her eyes. "He was nice enough, but I couldn't get rid of him. And did you see his top lip? He looked as if he'd just run a marathon, except he was too overweight to be a marathon runner."

Rhett chuckled. "Nice to know I could be of help."

Her lips curved up. "You like to think of yourself as a white knight, riding in to rescue the damsel in distress, don't you?"

He snorted. "You're perfectly able to handle yourself. I can't imagine you ever needing rescuing."

She smiled, but he thought he saw a touch of wistfulness in her eyes. That interested him. She'd always been incredibly independent, likely to slap him if he intimated she needed a man's help for anything. When they were together, if she'd been unable to open a jar, she'd have thrown it away and chosen something else rather than ask him to do it for her. Was she regretting being like that for so long? Maybe if she was struggling now, people were too wary of her reaction to offer her a helping hand.

He put the thought aside. It was none of his business. "Dinner?" he asked, offering her his arm the way Cary Grant might have done in the old days.

She laughed and slipped a hand into the crook of his elbow. "Sure. Lead on."

They entered the restaurant and found a couple of seats at a nearby table. Lisa was there, as was the man Neve had just been talking to, and for a moment Rhett worried he was taking part in a version of *A Midsummer Night's Dream*. In the end, though, it turned out to be a pleasant evening. Lisa was smart and funny, although she'd backed off after seeing him with Neve at morning tea. Scott, the guy Neve had been talking to, was opinionated but nice enough, and the others at the table were willing to join in the conversation.

Neve finally seemed to have relaxed in his company, and after a while the two of them slipped into their old routine, playing off each other's sense of humor and making the others laugh.

"I'm so glad this conference isn't one of those management courses," a guy was saying now. "You know, where you have to work out how to get a chicken, a fox, and a bag of rice across a river, or something."

"Yeah, I've been to those," Rhett said. "There was one where they told us we had to pretend the room was full of lava, and we only had a six foot plank to get from one side of the room to the other." He rolled his eyes.

"Did they ask you to lie down?" Neve asked.

He raised his eyebrows. "Are you saying I'm a six foot plank?"

"Clearly not, as you're five-eleven-and-three-quarters. But if the cap fits…"

He grinned, and she met his gaze, smiling back. They'd always been like this, teasing each other with an underlying sense of something more going on beneath the surface. He liked it. It warmed him through to know that maybe they'd finally be able to put their problems to one side. They might not have forgiven, or forgotten, what had happened, but perhaps it was possible to move on.

Next to her, Scott coughed. Rhett glanced at him and frowned. The man was sweating profusely, his face quite red, and he appeared to be having trouble breathing.

Rhett leaned forward. "Hey, Scott, are you okay?"

Neve turned to look at him, and she inhaled sharply. "Scott? What's the matter?"

The man shook his head, then rubbed his left arm. "Just a touch of cramp…"

Neve, however, got calmly to her feet and moved around to stand before him. She bent down and took his hand. "Scott, do you have any pain in your chest?"

He was breathing hard now. "A little… It's just indigestion, though. I've had it the last few days…"

"No, sweetie, I think you're having a heart attack." She looked straight at Rhett. "Can you tell Reception to ring for an ambulance, and see if they have any aspirin?"

"Of course." He stood and ran out into the foyer. There were two people behind Reception. He explained what had happened, and the woman immediately dialed the emergency services. The man picked up a first aid kit and followed Rhett back into the restaurant.

Scott was still at the table and appeared to be breathing, although he was obviously having difficulty.

"Should we give him CPR?" the man from reception asked, somewhat nervously.

"Not while he's breathing on his own." Neve was remarkably calm and in control. Like Rhett, she'd done a first aid course years ago, so she would have been aware of basic medical procedures. She rubbed Scott's shoulder lightly. "It's all right, honey, help's on the way. Are you allergic to aspirin that you know of?"

"No," Scott gasped.

Neve took a couple from the bottle that the receptionist found in the first aid box. "Crunch these," she instructed him, popping them into his mouth. "Don't swallow them—crunch them up."

He did so, taking deep gulps of breath as he did, groaning with pain.

Rhett loosened the man's tie and removed it, but he knew there was little more they could do other than to keep the guy comfortable until the ambulance arrived.

People were starting to look over, obviously realizing something was wrong.

"Oh God," Scott groaned. "Everyone's staring."

Neve placed herself in front of him, blocking his view of the room. "Don't you worry about anyone else," she stated firmly. "Concentrate on me. You're going to be fine, okay? Nice calm breaths, now. Is there anyone we can telephone for you?"

"My wife," Scott gasped. "Her number's on my phone."

To be fair to her, Neve didn't bat an eyelid, even though the guy had been chatting her up half the evening. She handed his phone to Lisa, who found his wife's number and walked away to call her.

Neve continued talking softly to him, rubbing his hand reassuringly, until the ambulance arrived. Only then did she step back and let them take over.

It took them about five minutes to get him onto a stretcher, make sure he was comfortable, and load him into the ambulance, and then they were off to the hospital, the siren fading into the snowy night.

Everyone returned to the restaurant, people milling around like they always did whenever there was an emergency, full of a need to discuss it and comfort each other even if they hadn't been part of the event.

Neve stood to one side, though, and shook her head as Rhett walked up to her.

"Jesus." She ran her hands through her dark hair, and Rhett saw that her hands were shaking.

"You all right?" He touched her shoulder.

"I need a fucking drink." She turned away and walked out of the room.

Pursing his lips, Rhett followed her.

Chapter Seven

Neve walked up to the bar and leaned on the counter as she surveyed the wines available in the fridge behind the barman.

Rhett appeared at her side and rested next to her, his arm an inch from hers. "Did you finish your meal?"

"Not quite, but I don't want to go back in there with everyone gawping." She ran her hand through her hair, feeling queasy. "I can't believe I mocked him for being sweaty. That poor man."

She wasn't sure what Rhett's reaction would be, half expecting him to scold her for ridiculing the man, half anticipating him to say she was being self-centered for worrying about her own feelings after the guy had been carried off.

He did neither, though. His lips curved up, and he surveyed her with what looked like genuine affection. "You're such a puzzle," he said. "Full of contrasts. You can be sharp as a knife, and yet nobody could have comforted Scott better than how you just did. You have a heart of gold, Neve Clark. I just wish you'd realize it and start feeling better about yourself."

It was such a strange thing to say that she stared at him, but he'd turned his attention to the barman and was busy ordering a bottle of Mac's Gold.

"Um, a glass of the Marlborough Pinot Gris please," she said when Rhett gestured to her. She'd thought about asking for a brandy, but didn't want to go straight for the hard stuff in front of him.

Wait, why not? She caught the thought even as it passed through her mind. Since when did she care what Rhett thought of her? What business was it of his what she drank?

She was tempted to change her order, but the barman had already started pouring the wine, so she closed her mouth and resolved to order a Cognac next.

Her heart had begun to slow its frenetic hammering on her ribs, and as she relaxed a little she became more aware of the man next to her, her senses slowly reacting to his presence like a flower turning to the sun.

He'd always had this effect on her. He seemed to affect her at a cellular level, as if subtle, chemical changes occurred whenever he was close, her hormones reacting to his. Aftershave was one of the few things he'd spent money on when they were together, and she suspected his current one was also expensive. She couldn't help but lean a little closer and inhale the woody, spicy fragrance with a touch of vanilla.

"You smell nice," she said as he looked at her.

"Thank you. You too." He smiled.

She frowned and wrinkled her nose. "It has a strange base note… is it… rum?"

He laughed. "Yeah. I love it. It makes me feel like a pirate."

Neve's lips curved up at his joke, but to her, even in wintry Queenstown, it smelled of the tropics, of warm, sultry nights and skin sliding against damp skin beneath silky bedclothes.

Swallowing hard, she looked down at where he leaned on the bar. He'd removed his jacket and rolled up his shirt sleeves earlier in the evening, and his forearms were tanned and scattered with light brown hairs, still bearing the distinctive strong muscles he'd developed during his sporting days. Her fingers itched to reach out and run along that tanned skin, to slide along the crisp shirt where it had tightened on his biceps, and to feel the hard muscle she knew lay beneath. He had a tattoo that curled around his left upper arm—she could see it faintly through the white cotton of his shirt, dark thorns twisting around the muscle in a pattern that acknowledged his father's Maori lineage. Neve had lain in bed and traced it occasionally while he was asleep. It was like her secret symbol on a semi-intimate place others might have seen but only she got to touch.

It wasn't hers to touch any longer, though. She averted her gaze, accepted the glass of wine from the barman, and took a big gulp, feeling a bit shaky.

"Come on," Rhett said. "Let's sit down before you fall down."

"I'm perfectly fine," she protested, but she let him take her arm and lead her across to a table in the corner, away from prying eyes.

"Are you trying to seduce me into your lair?" she mumbled, sliding along the bench.

He slid beside her, giving her a wry look. "I'm trying to make sure you don't pass out and hit your head on the bar. I think one ambulance a night is enough for any hotel."

"I wouldn't dream of fainting. Fainting's for girls."

He gave a short laugh. "Drink your wine, then I'm getting you a brandy."

"I don't want a brandy."

"Drink the fucking wine, Neve, and then I'll order you a Cognac because I know you want one."

She had a mouthful of wine, glaring sulkily at the table.

He swigged his beer and chuckled. "Don't pout."

"I'm not pouting."

He sighed. "Jeez."

"What?"

"You're in that sort of mood."

"What sort of mood?"

"In nineteenth century English novels they'd have called it contrary. Disagreeing with everything I say."

"No I'm not."

She met his gaze, and they both laughed. Warmth slid down inside her that wasn't entirely due to the Pinot Gris. In one way it was infuriating to know she'd changed so little that he could read her just as well as he always had.

But in another way there was something nice about having a shared history. On an ordinary date, she felt as if she were acting, playing the role of successful, sexy business woman, saying the things she knew she had to say on a date to keep a guy's interest, being spirited but not too outrageous if she didn't want to frighten him off. But with Rhett she didn't have to pretend. He already knew all her weaknesses, all her faults.

Holding up her wine glass, she gave a toast, "To the past."

He met her gaze. Perhaps it was the wine she'd already drunk, or the sultry scent of his aftershave, or maybe it was just the look in his eyes, but a shiver ran down her spine, and she felt her nipples tighten in her bra.

"To the future," he said.

What did he mean by that? Was he saying he didn't want to think about their past?

Or was he suggesting something might happen between them later?

She blinked. Of course he wasn't. He knew as well as she did that any chance of a relationship had long since vanished into the distance. He was just saying he'd put the past behind him, and he'd moved on.

"To the future," she said and clinked her glass against his bottle.

As she sipped her wine, though, she couldn't summon any positive feelings about her future. Not her personal one, anyway. But wasn't that why she was here? She'd decided to put her love life to one side for a while and concentrate on her business. Rhett turning up had muddied the waters a little, but she had to remember her focus for being there.

She leaned back on the bench and blew out a long, slow breath. "Poor Scott. I hope he's going to be okay."

"Yeah, it wasn't a great way to finish the first day."

She scratched at a mark on the table. "I do feel bad for mocking him."

"Well, you weren't to know he was ill. He was pretty opinionated, and he had been chatting you up while he had a wife back home. Having a heart attack doesn't make him a saint."

"I suppose not. But I want to feel bad. Stop trying to make me feel good."

He chuckled. "All right."

She took another large gulp of wine. Her hands were still shaking a little—had he noticed?

"I heard from Hitch earlier," he said. "He's got a new commission somewhere in the South American jungle."

"Oh, nice."

"Yeah, he was pleased."

"Rowan will enjoy being taken up the Amazon, I'm sure."

Rhett coughed into his beer and then shook his head as he wiped his mouth. "I think beer came out of my nose then."

"I know you won't believe me, but I didn't actually mean that to sound as rude as it did," she said, amused at his reaction.

They both laughed and then studied each other with some fondness and affection, on his part as well as hers, she thought. If only she could erase the black cloud of that terrible argument they'd had, which hung over her so ominously.

"About what happened when we broke up…" she began softly.

But he put a finger to his lips and gave her a warning glance. "Let's not talk about the past. It's done, Neve. It's water under the bridge. Let's look upstream and see what's coming, not behind us at what's gone."

She looked away, out of the window. The street lamp illuminated the falling snow, turning it gold against the backdrop of the dark night.

"I don't know that I can," she whispered. "How do you let go of the past when it sticks to you like Velcro?"

"Tell me what's been happening over the last few years," he suggested. "What have you been up to?"

Outside, a couple strolled hand-in-hand. As they reached the lamp, the guy turned the girl toward him and kissed her, a long, lingering embrace that made the hairs rise up on the back of Neve's neck. She averted her gaze, turning it back to her glass of wine on the table. Observing other people's happiness only seemed to highlight her own melancholy.

"Working on the business mainly," she said. She forced herself to think of the Four Seasons and how far they'd come. As usual, it gave her a lift to think of their hard work and what they'd created. "I don't think any of us expected it to have turned out so well. We all knew we'd put in a hundred percent, but new businesses go under every day."

"Rowan's designs must have filled some kind of gap in the market to be so popular," he said.

"I think so. There's lots of gorgeous lingerie out there, but much of it is really expensive. We've tried to combine beauty and comfort with affordability. And although we offer all sizes, we've worked really hard to try to produce underwear that's especially comfortable and well fitting for ladies with generous figures like the four of us."

Rhett's eyebrows rose. "You girls are hardly overweight."

"Maybe not, but what became clear to us is that no two woman are built the same, and just saying something is a size twelve doesn't really mean anything. We don't exactly make to measure, but Rowan's very clever at designing bras, for example, that emphasize the good bits and hide the not-so-good."

"Are there any not-so-good?"

Neve grinned. "All women are conscious of their figures. We all have an extra inch or more that we don't want to draw attention to. And she's good at disguising with dark colors and emphasizing with bright. Color plays a big part in her work."

"I'd be happy to see some samples," he said. "Give you my opinion."

His lips held a little curve, and his eyes shone in the warm light of the bar. Again, she felt a frisson pass through her. Was he flirting with her? In any other case, she would have said definitely, but suddenly she felt like a teenager again, confused by signals and afraid of making a fool of herself.

She'd half forgotten, but now she remembered he'd always made her feel like that. He might not be a physically overpowering guy—he wasn't built like Hitch, six foot three with shoulders that looked as if he still had his coat hanger in his jacket—but there was something charismatic and seductive about Rhett that was just as masculine, and that somehow made her feel very... feminine.

She finished off her wine, aware her hand was shaking, although now she thought it probably wasn't from shock.

"'I'll get you a brandy," Rhett said, and he stood and went over to the bar.

Irritation flared within her briefly that he hadn't asked what she'd wanted and had assumed, but the fact was that she did want a Cognac, so she held her peace and instead just watched him as he ordered their drinks.

He was so different from when they'd lived together. Different hair, different aftershave, different clothes. And his manner seemed different too, as if all the anger had been drained out of him. She wasn't sure how she felt about that. His anger, his hot temper, had made him exciting. He'd lived life at a million miles an hour, barely sitting still at all. It was as if there had been something within him burning to get out, a supernova shining so bright it had encompassed everything around it.

Sometimes she'd felt caught in its glare, as if she were a planet orbiting around his sun. That had been frustrating at times, and his natural inclination to take charge and organize everything—including her—had caused quite a few fights. But it had also made them explosive in the bedroom. She'd been relatively inexperienced before she'd met him, having slept with only a couple of guys that had been mainly fumbling around in the dark. Sex with Rhett had been a revelation. A little shy at first, she'd soon lost her reticence as he'd encouraged her to try new positions and different techniques. He'd been dominant without being forceful, insatiable all the time, which had suited her fine because she hadn't been able to get enough of him.

And now? Without that fire inside him, would he be the same in bed? She wondered why his anger had dissipated. Was it just because he'd matured and lost the impatience of youth? Was it the shock of losing his father? Or was it connected to his own illness? She didn't know much about testicular cancer, but she guessed what treatment he'd had must have affected his sex life.

Could he still have children? She watched him say something to the barman, who laughed, and then pick up the drinks before turning toward her. They'd been too young to talk about having a family when they were together. She wasn't even sure he wanted kids.

It made her sad to think of how much they'd changed. Growing up wasn't half as fun as everyone made it out to be.

Chapter Eight

Rhett placed Neve's Cognac in front of her and slid back onto the bench. He'd ordered himself a Scotch, and he took a mouthful of it and enjoyed the burn down into his stomach.

Neve sipped at her Cognac. She was still pale, and she looked sad, although her face had lit up when she'd talked about her business.

"So you're the Marketing Manager at Four Seasons," he stated. He'd picked up that much from the conversations he'd overheard when he'd joined their friends occasionally for a drink. "Tell me a bit about that."

She explained how she was responsible for marketing and promotion of the business. She booked them into fashion shows, helped with the shop displays, and organized advertising.

"Sounds great," he said. "Liam also said you host parties, is that right? That's an innovative way of spreading the word."

"Yeah." An impish look crossed her face. "At a seminar a few years ago I met a woman who was marketing manager for… another company, and we decided we could work together."

"What sort of company?"

"Sex toys." She tried not to laugh and failed, collapsing into a bout of giggles. "You should see your face."

He grinned, relieved to see her sadness lift for once. "I see. So it's *that* sort of party."

She shrugged, still laughing. "It's just a bit of fun. Women are less inhibited when men aren't there. Often they're not brave enough to go into a sex shop, and even going into a lingerie shop can be daunting if you feel you're on the big side and are worried other women are going to judge you because of the way you look. When friends are together, though, they tend to dare each other to try things. We usually hold the parties at someone's house on a Friday night, charge ten bucks per person to cover snacks and petrol, everyone brings a bottle of wine, we put on some dance music, and we usually have fun too. It's all about increasing exposure, isn't it?"

Thinking about exposure brought to mind Neve stripping for him and gradually revealing the sexy underwear he was convinced lay beneath her clothing. What with that and her mention of sex toys, now he was getting all hot under the collar.

"Stop thinking about me naked," she said. "That's not allowed."

"Oh, you think I'm that easy to read?"

"You're a man. Of course you're easy to read."

"Ouch."

"Deny it then."

He couldn't, because he had, and they both laughed.

"This is nice," he said. "This is all I wanted. Just to be able to talk to you. I miss that."

"As I recall," she said, "we didn't talk a whole lot."

He chuckled. "Yes, we did. In between."

"Yeah. I suppose we did." She sipped her brandy, inhaled deeply, and blew out a breath, a little more tension visibly leaving her shoulders.

"Do you still play badminton?" It was a question that he'd wanted to ask for a while, but hadn't had the courage to broach.

"Only socially." Her hand strayed to her right shoulder, almost subconsciously, he thought. "The girls and I were in Christchurch when the earthquake hit in 2011. We were right in the town center. As we tried to make our way out of the city, a wall next to us collapsed and a heavy lump of concrete landed on my shoulder. It put paid to any badminton career I might have had."

"Oh, Jesus." He hadn't known. "I'm so sorry to hear that."

She shrugged and dropped her hand. "By then I'd pretty much given up, anyway." She shook her head, as if to say she didn't want to talk about it anymore. "Do you mind if I ask you more about your illness?"

He swirled the amber liquid over the ice in his glass. "Ask away."

"When you had the operation, did they just remove the cancer?"

"No. I had an orchiectomy. The whole testicle was removed."

She winced. "Ouch."

"Yeah. It's called inguinal—the incision's made here." He drew a short line across his abdomen, below his belt.

"So you can't wear a bikini anymore?"

He laughed. "No."

"Did you have an... um... implant? Like a woman who has a breast removed?"

"No. They offered one, but I read around the net and generally the advice is not to unless you're bothered by it. You can't see that it's been removed—you'd have to purposely feel it to know. And anyway, my jeans don't pinch in the crotch like they used to."

"So that's one good thing that's come out of it."

"Yeah." He grinned.

She looked into her glass, chewing her bottom lip.

He smiled. "Ask me, Neve."

"Ask you what?"

"Whatever you're itching to ask."

Her cool blue eyes studied him. "Can you still have children?"

That completely surprised him. He'd assumed she was going to ask if he could still get an erection, or ejaculate. "Ah, yes. Should be able to, anyway. The other testicle takes over the production of sperm, and usually the sperm count stays the same. The wonder of nature. I did bank some sperm under their advice, just in case, but hopefully I won't need it."

She nodded and sipped her brandy. What was she thinking, and why had she asked that? Sheer curiosity?

They studied each other quietly for a moment, drinking and listening to the sounds of the bar—the tinkle of glasses, the murmured conversation; quiet, reassuring sounds of people enjoying each other's company.

"Do you think it's changed you much?" Neve asked.

"In what way?"

"In any way."

He thought about it. "I don't know. Maybe. It was a difficult year, especially with Dad dying." He decided to be honest. "It took quite a lot of... adjustment, I suppose. I grew up a lot. Cancer is a disease we don't tend to think about when we're in our twenties. It's a scary word, and it's difficult not to think of it as fatal, even though more and more people are surviving it nowadays."

"That's true."

"But testicular cancer hits a guy right where it hurts, you know? Emotionally and physically. Once you've got over the initial shock and accepted it's treatable, it raises a whole hoard of other questions. What will it look like after the op? Am I going to feel self-conscious in front of girls? What will my sex life be like? Can I still get it up? Can I ejaculate? Can I have kids? Will it change me in other ways? What about hormones? Am I going to grow boobs?"

Her lips curved up briefly, but her face had paled again. "It must have been awful for you."

He shrugged and took another big mouthful of whisky. It had been the lowest point of his life. Losing Neve had been the only thing that had come close to it.

"It passed," he said, "like all things do in time."

She nodded, but he had the feeling she didn't agree. From the things she'd said since they'd met that morning, he was beginning to think she hadn't moved on the way he had. She didn't even seem to have grown any older. She styled her hair the same way, wore the same perfume, and so far her attitude seemed to be the same. She was talking to him, but he knew she hadn't forgiven him for what had happened all those years ago.

The only thing different about her was that she looked beaten, he thought. It was as if they used to travel from one city to another every day on the same train that was repeatedly held up by work being done on the line. He'd finally decided to go by bike, and even though the journey was harder, he'd discovered new landscapes and people along the way. But Neve had continued to take the train, too stubborn to change, and depressing herself when, every day, she found the same problems on the line, and the same delays.

He didn't want to be one of the things that made her sadder. He wanted to see her eyes light up again. If he couldn't do that for longer than a few seconds at a time, he might as well call a day to this and go up to his room.

"I can, by the way," he said.

"Can what?" She raised her glass to her lips.

"Get it up and ejaculate."

She swallowed too much Cognac in one go and had a coughing fit. Rhett laughed as she tried to calm herself, eventually getting up to fetch her a glass of water.

"Sorry," she wheezed after drinking half the glass. "Jeez, I wasn't expecting that."

He grinned. "I wanted to lighten the mood."

"You've certainly done that, all right." She wiped her mouth, unable to hide a smile. "Well, thanks for sharing that with me."

"You're welcome."

"I'm guessing you've not just tested whether the equipment works on your own?"

"Ah, no. I had help."

"Anyone serious?"

"Not since the op, no."

"Before?"

So she wasn't just interested in the operation. She wanted to know if he'd fallen in love with anyone else.

He rested an elbow on the back of the bench and leaned his head on a hand. The whisky was beginning to have an effect, filing away the edges, sanding him smooth. Was Neve feeling the same way? She'd always been able to hold her drink, but it had tended to loosen her up and strip away the metal railings and barbed wire she erected around herself that yelled *Keep Away!*

"There was one girl," he admitted. "Sarah. I met her in Australia. We dated for about six months."

Neve mirrored his pose, leaning her head on her hand, and studied his face. She didn't look jealous or resentful, just wistful. "What was she like?"

"Completely the opposite to you."

"She was beautiful, intelligent, and witty, then?"

He smiled at her self-deprecating comment, thinking how those three words could easily have described Neve. "She's blonde. Quiet. Very gentle, on herself and on others. Restful, I suppose."

Neve nodded. "She sounds nice."

"She was."

"But you broke up?"

"When I came back to New Zealand. We keep in touch by phone and on Facebook, that kind of thing."

"Does she know about your cancer?"

He hesitated. He'd said to Neve earlier that he hadn't told anyone about it except his mother and sister. If he told the truth now, he'd be admitting he'd lied back then.

He didn't want to lie anymore, though, so he nodded.

Neve swallowed and lowered her gaze. "Right."

"It doesn't mean anything," he said softly. "She wanted to know why I'd made the decision not to continue with the badminton."

"You didn't consider moving back to Australia to be with her?"

"I considered it."

"Why didn't you?"

He tipped his head from side to side. "I liked her a lot. But I didn't feel what I was sure a man's supposed to feel for someone he wants to make a commitment with."

He waited for her to ask whether he'd felt that way with her, but she didn't.

"What about you?" he asked. "Has there been anyone special?"

She turned her glass around in her fingers. "A couple I liked more than others."

That suggested she'd had a few lovers along the way, which was what Liam had implied too. It saddened Rhett, but not necessarily because he resented her sleeping with other men—he didn't like to think about it, but she wasn't his anymore, and she owed him no loyalty. He felt sad because he was beginning to think she'd done the same as him—tried repeatedly to find someone to replace him, without any luck.

Not for the first time, he wondered how her parents had reacted to their breakup. Bella Clark had been lovely, but she couldn't have been more different to the spirited Neve. She was much more like her other daughter, Deana—placid and non-confrontational, doing anything to avoid an argument and to have a quiet life. Brian Clark had been a piece of work, almost Victorian in his attitude about his place as head of the household. A strict Catholic, he'd brought his daughters up the same way, sending them both to an all girls' boarding school that Deana had tolerated but Neve had abhorred. Through every one of her teenage years, Neve had rebelled. Once she'd left home to go to university, Brian had obviously realized he had no control over her anymore, but it hadn't stopped him voicing his opinions on how she should live her life. He'd disapproved vociferously when she'd moved in with Rhett, although Rhett himself had gotten on okay with the guy when they were on their own. Oddly, that had always annoyed him, because it implied that Brian thought it acceptable for a guy to want to sleep with a girl before marriage but completely unacceptable for the girl to want to do so.

"How's your dad?" he asked.

She pushed her glass toward him. "Get us another one and I might tell you how bad it's gotten."

"Ah. Sure." He stood.

"Put them on my bill this time, will you? Room 134."

"Okay." He took their glasses and went up to the bar, his heart racing a little. Had telling him her room number been completely innocent? Or was there some subtext beneath it?

He requested two of the same from the barman and leaned on the bar, staring at the polished wood. What if there was subtext? What did it mean?

Clearly, her relationship with her father was worse than it had ever been. Instead of leaving the safety of her castle to meet her fears, life had forced her to shore up her defenses and defend more than ever. She would never forgive Rhett for leaving, and he was stupid if he thought there was any chance she'd relax enough to have a fun brief fling while they were away.

And yet... He glanced over his shoulder to see her with her head still propped on a hand, watching him. She didn't look away as he met her gaze, or look embarrassed at having been caught staring. Instead, her lips curved up in a lazy smile.

Rhett shivered and turned his attention to telling the barman what room number to put the drinks on. 134. Her mention of the number had been related to the bill, nothing more.

Hadn't it?

Chapter Nine

Neve watched him walk back and place her brandy before her. The first Cognac had done its job, and her hands had finally stopped shaking. Her shoulders had loosened, and it seemed easier to breathe. She didn't want to drink too much, but she liked the way the alcohol helped her relax. It didn't erase the past, but it did seem to help her get things in perspective, and she no longer felt the need to keep up her guard. Rhett wasn't the enemy. He was a decent guy, and he still seemed to care for her, which felt nice after so much time feeling lost and alone.

He slid back in beside her, this time settling closer than before, his knee brushing hers. The barman had turned off the overhead lights and flicked on the smaller, more intimate lamps on the walls. Joss Stone was singing *Got a Right to be Wrong* softly in the background, and the roaring log fire, along with the smell of Rhett's aftershave, made her forget how cold and wintry it was outside. It reminded her of the hot summer they'd spent together back in the day. They'd travelled up to the Northland for a week over Christmas and had stayed in a bach on Ninety Mile Beach, and they'd spent the days swimming, surfing, and eating fish and chips on the beach, and the nights growing hot and sticky under the sheets, teasing pleasure from each other as slowly as they could bear.

Rhett took a mouthful of whisky, and she watched his Adam's apple dip and his throat contract as he swallowed. He ran his tongue around his lips to catch any drops he might have missed, and it made her shiver and clench deep inside at the memory of his mouth on hers, on her breasts, between her legs.

She lifted her gaze to his. His eyes were warm, and she suspected he'd read her mind. He didn't look angry though. He looked as if he was thinking exactly the same thing.

"So," he said. "You were going to tell me about your dad."

"Oh, yeah." She didn't want to think about that Christmas, she wanted to think about the one she'd spent with Rhett, but she'd said she'd tell him what had happened, and besides he knew what her father was like. He'd always been on her side whenever she'd had trouble in the past. Would he be the same now?

She studied her glass, turning it around and admiring the mahogany-colored liquid that glowed in the firelight. Without looking up, she told him what had happened on Christmas Day. Rhett remained quiet while she spoke, but when she repeated her father's words to her about keeping her mouth and legs closed, she looked up to see his eyes blazing with fury.

"Fucking cheek," he said.

She felt a rush of relief that made her blink away sudden tears. "I haven't seen him since. Mum's upset and Deana said I'm just making things worse."

"That's bullshit. She should back you up, for fuck's sake, not criticize you for it."

Neve swallowed hard. "Thank you."

"For what?"

"For seeing my side of things." She rubbed her nose and sipped her brandy. "It was such a horrible thing to say. I know I speak my mind, but I don't think I'm nasty with it. And as for the other thing..." She scratched at a mark on the table. "I haven't been with that many guys."

"Neve, I don't care if you've slept with a hundred men. Well, I do—my point is that it's irrelevant, and it's none of your father's business."

She looked up at him, unable to stop her lips curving. "You do care?"

His slow smile matched hers. "Yes, I care. Does that surprise you?"

She gave a little shrug.

He tipped his head to the side. "Can you say honestly that it doesn't bother you to think about me with someone else?"

She dropped her gaze for a moment. Another girl touching him, kissing him, going down on him, having him inside her... She swallowed hard and looked back up. "Yes, it bothers me."

His gaze slid to her mouth. "Does it help if I tell you that you were the best? That none of them compared to you?"

Emotion washed over her, strong enough to make tears sting her eyes again. Jeez, she was going to bawl her eyes out before the end of the evening at this rate. What was wrong with her? She never cried easily. It must have been dealing with Scott, she thought, and finding out Rhett had had cancer.

But it wasn't really that. She felt emotional because he'd told her none of the women he'd been with had compared to her, and that was such a sweet thing to hear that she knew it would warm her through for many days to come.

"Are you going to cry on me, Clark? I might need to get out my camera to capture the moment, if that's the case."

"Not likely," she said with a sniff.

He grinned and had another swallow of whisky. "So what are you going to do about your dad?"

"Hell knows. Right at this moment, I don't care if I never see him again." They were brave words, and she was still too angry to consider forgiving him, but she couldn't deny to herself the pain she felt inside. She missed him, and her mother. "Jeez. It's so bloody hard." She sighed.

Rhett glanced down at his crotch. "That's a bit personal."

She chuckled. "Honestly. It always comes back to sex with you, doesn't it?"

He rested his head on a hand. "Always." His eyes glowed.

A delicious shiver ran down her back. *Be careful*, the angel whispered on her left shoulder, but she didn't want to be careful, not right at that moment. Being there, in his company, felt decadent and wicked, as if she'd sat down for dinner having ordered an enormous ice cream sundae and nothing else. He was so goddamn sexy, and all she could think about was how it had felt to make love with him. He'd understood that sometimes she'd wanted it slow and lingering, at other times hard and fast, and he'd always obliged, never failing to give her at least one orgasm.

"Tell me about your parties," he said.

She raised her eyebrows. "What about them?"

"I'm intrigued. I can't imagine how it works. Do you have to do… demonstrations?"

Her eyes widened. "You mean with the sex toys?"

"Yeah."

She pursed her lips. He was such a naughty boy. "Turn you on, does it? The thought of me performing for a group of women?"

He shrugged and grinned. "I can't imagine there's any guy wouldn't be turned on by that."

"You're shocking," she said, loving every minute. He'd always had a kinky side she'd adored.

"So, do you?"

"As much fun as I think it would be to pretend I did, no, I don't. Not like that, anyway. I do take them out of the packaging and show how they work, though."

He had another swallow of whisky. He was loosening up, too. They were letting go of the social rules and regulations that normally bound them, forgetting what they should and shouldn't say, ignoring what was acceptable and right and decent, and instead acting purely on instinct, removed from everything but the fact that they were just a man and woman.

"What sort of things?" he asked. "Any we would have used back in the day?"

His eyes had lit with pleasure—he was enjoying talking like this too. He still wanted her. She could see it in his gaze, hear it in his voice. He wouldn't be saying these things if he wasn't hoping they'd end the evening in the same room.

At that realization, her heart gave a little leap. Holy shit. Was she really considering going to bed with him again?

Nothing could ever alter the past. Like her father, he would never say he was sorry, and she would always have to live with the memory of that final argument, that overwhelming sense of betrayal.

But that didn't belong here. Not in this cozy room, with the snow still falling outside, soft jazz playing in the background, the taste of brandy in her mouth, the smell of his aftershave rich and warm in the air. It was as if time had slowed and a bubble had descended to cover the room, isolating them from everyone else in the hotel—until all that existed was this table, this bench, and the man beside her. His eyes told her he wasn't going to pressure her, but if she wanted him, he was there, and he'd be more than happy to take her not only up to his room but to heaven and back—probably more than once, knowing him.

She moistened her lips with the tip of her tongue, not missing the way his gaze dropped to watch. If she slept with him again, there would be no going back. She wouldn't be able to undo that moment. It would be a file in her memory banks that would have to remain there forever, flashing up on the screen inside her mind to torture her and remind her of the stupid mistake she'd made.

Did it have to be a stupid mistake? Did everything have to be measured by an apocalyptic scale? Or was it possible that they could share one night, one moment, and that it could be sexy and nice and pleasant, like eating that huge chocolate sundae, without having to deal with the guilt that always seemed to accompany an indulgence afterward? Rhett wasn't a nasty piece of work like some of the men she'd met. He wasn't out to punish her, or prove a point. He liked her. He cared for her.

Does it help if I tell you that you were the best? That none of them compared to you?

It made her want to cry.

She swallowed her emotion down with another glug of brandy. No decisions had been made yet, no barriers crossed. She could stop this at any time. Flirting with him didn't mean they had to have sex, and he wasn't the sort of guy who'd get angry if she changed her mind later. He knew the stakes, and he'd know what a step it would be for her—for both of them, even if she tried to tell herself it wasn't a momentous move.

She wasn't going to think about it. She was going to live in the moment, and enjoy herself for once.

"Mmm… what sort of things?" She tapped her forefinger against her lips. Then she giggled. "Actually, I have something in my suitcase we would have had great fun with."

His lips curved up. "You brought it with you?"

"I did. I was going to… try it out while I was away." She laughed as he blew out a breath.

"Go on then," he said. "Tell me more."

"It's a vibrator that sort of clips on—it's a bit difficult to describe. Suffice to say it hits all the right areas apparently. That's what I was going to check out this week."

He nodded his approval. "You'll have to let me know how it turns out."

She nibbled her bottom lip. "That's not all of it. The best bit is that it's remote controlled."

His eyebrows slowly rose again. "Whoa."

"Yeah. The girl's partner can control it using an app on his—or her—phone."

"What a great idea."

"It would be wonderful for phone sex or Skype sex," she said.

"Mmm." His eyes appraised her, hot, interested. "I'm glad to hear you still enjoy… experimenting."

She shrugged. "It's not so much fun on your own. I haven't been with a guy for ages."

"Why not?"

She dunked a piece of ice in her glass with a finger. "Don't know. The novelty wore off, I guess."

"You're bored with sex?"

She met his gaze again, amused. "Not quite." She slid down on the bench a little, resting her head on the back. She felt warm and relaxed, as if she'd been made of metal, but had been turned into plastic that had been softened by the fire. "I suppose I realized that good sex isn't just physical."

"Orgasms don't hold the same thrill they used to?"

She nudged him with her elbow. "I meant that bedroom gymnastics don't amount to much if you don't have feelings for the guy. I tried to convince myself it was possible to replicate what we had with just anyone. That was stupid." She was almost talking to herself now. "When we were together, I didn't realize there was a difference between sex and making love. I thought it was the same thing. It's just body parts, right? One bit going into another. Touch the buttons in the right order and you get the reward. But it doesn't work like that. Or at least, the reward isn't as…"

"Satisfying," he said.

"Yeah." She lifted her gaze to his. His smile had faded, and he looked… wistful. "Do you feel the same?" she whispered.

"I told you, you were the best. No other woman has ever compared to you, Neve. I don't mean in terms of technique—although you were top of the list there, too. I mean in terms of connection. I've never felt for anyone what I felt for you."

"Too bad that wasn't enough to keep us together," she whispered.

He tipped his head to the side. "Maybe then it wasn't. We were so young back then. I don't want to think about it. It makes me sad. I want to think about now. It's warm and cozy in here, and we're finally talking, and I still get that tingle when you look at me, Neve Clark. It gives me the warm fuzzies right down to my toes. Doesn't it you?"

Chapter Ten

Rhett let his words settle on Neve like the snow outside. He felt as if the world had stopped spinning and all the birds and animals and people were holding their breath, awaiting her reaction.

At any point, he expected her to toss an insult at him, *Who do you think you are, Rhett Taylor?* And to walk away with her chin in the air. She'd been angry with him for so long that he couldn't imagine she'd ever be able to let her disappointment and resentment go.

But her eyes were wistful, and he could see his words had touched her.

He didn't want to talk about the past. He wanted to concentrate on that moment, on how it felt to sit next to the woman who'd haunted his dreams for so long, and on the promise that glittered in her eyes.

She lowered her gaze then, looking at her hand where it rested in her lap. "I don't know what to say. I know the old Rhett so well, in many ways, and yet I don't know the new one at all."

"He's not so different." He smiled.

"My guard has been up for so long, I'm scared about letting it down," she whispered. "I want to. Being here, with you… I feel better than I've felt in months. Years even. I've missed you so much, Rhett."

He could only imagine the courage it had taken for her to admit that. "Aw. I've missed you too."

"How do we know we're not making a mistake, though?" Fear shone in her eyes.

"Life doesn't come with a guarantee, nor does love, unfortunately. Neither of us planned this. I don't know what's going to happen in the next minute, let alone the next hour. All I do know is that having cancer has taught me to appreciate every moment of my life, and to make the most of any opportunities that come my way. I would never have believed we'd be sitting here like this. I feel like it's my birthday and Christmas rolled into one."

She gave a soft laugh and looked up at him, into his eyes. "It's so strange, being like this after all that time."

He shifted an inch closer to her. Now their thighs brushed, and she was almost in the circle of his arms. If he bent his head, he'd be able to kiss her injured shoulder. More than anything, he wanted to remove her jumper, slip off her blouse, and place his lips there, but he had to content himself with looking at her for now.

Feeling brave, he reached out for her hand. She still had the hands of someone who'd played a lot of sports—with strong wrists and flexible fingers, her nails short, neatly painted with a French manicure. They were cool in his, and she inhaled as he brushed his thumb across her knuckles. Odd, he thought, how such an innocent gesture could feel so intimate when you've been alone a long time. Shaking hands or accepting a bear hug from a mate, or kissing a girl on the cheek, didn't satisfy this human need to touch and be touched.

He lifted her hand, placed their palms together, and spread his fingers, and hers automatically curled to lace between his. He couldn't stop himself lifting them to his lips and pressing a kiss on the tips.

Neve didn't say anything, but as she reached for her drink and finished it off, he was pleased that some color had returned to her cheeks, and her hands had stopped shaking. He could still see wariness in her eyes, though, and he didn't like that. He didn't know where tonight was heading, but by the end of the evening he wanted to see her eyes filled with affection and, maybe, desire, and nothing else. He didn't want to get her drunk by any means—there was no fun in seducing an incoherent woman. If that was what he was doing. Was he seducing her? He wasn't sure. That hadn't been his intention. He'd just wanted to get her talking to him. But he was enjoying himself, and he didn't want the evening to end yet.

He replaced her hand in her lap. "Another brandy?"

"Go on then. One more."

He rose and went over to the bar to order, waited for the drinks, and returned to sit beside her, sliding on the seat until he was back in the same position. When she didn't object, he held out his hand again. With a little smile, she placed hers back in it.

"Talk to me," he said, having a sip of the whisky and replacing the glass on the table. "What else have you been up to? Have you been away on holiday?"

"Birdie and I went to China last year," she said. "You went there for a tournament once, didn't you?"

There didn't seem to be animosity behind her question, so he was happy to admit, "Yes. In Beijing."

"Did you get to see much of the country?"

"Yeah, after the tournament I traveled with one of the other squad members for a week or so. What was your favorite place?"

They talked about the Forbidden City and the Temple of Heaven, and how different the culture was there, and then went on to discuss other places they'd been to. She told him about her visit to Rome and how much she'd loved the Sistine Chapel. He described Seoul and how he'd been to Lotte World, the world's second largest indoor theme park, and screamed all the way around the French Revolution roller coaster, making her laugh.

From time to time they mentioned people they'd traveled with, including past partners, but as the evening wore on, he felt as if they were both coming to terms with the time that had passed, and the fact that, like boats sailing on a lake, they'd parted ways and had now circled back to meet each other again.

They talked about everything under the sun—movies they'd watched, books they'd read, their friends and families, even what food they'd discovered on their travels. Rhett didn't ever want to stop, but eventually Neve fell quiet, and he knew the evening was coming to an end.

It wasn't late by any means—only ten o'clock, and he wasn't drunk—but the lights seemed to have a haze around them, and he felt as if he'd had an hour-long massage, every muscle in his body warm and relaxed.

Music had been playing all evening in the background, blues and jazz numbers from both past and present. Now the song changed to a rather cheesy ballad, but it was one he remembered dancing to with her many years before.

Unable to stop his lips curving up, he rose from the bench, walked around the table, and held out his hand.

She stared at it, then glanced around the bar. Nobody else was dancing.

"Seriously?" she said.

"I want you in my arms," he stated. "And this is a decent way to start the process."

She met his gaze and pressed her lips together, then grinned and let him pull her to her feet. He led her into the space between two tables, held her right hand with his left, rested the other on her waist, and they started to move.

"Everybody's staring," she whispered, her gaze flicking around the room.

"I don't give a fuck." All he could think about was the warm, soft woman pressed against him. She wore her sexy black high heels, bringing her almost up to his height, but not quite. If he were to lean closer, he could press his lips on the bridge of her nose. So he did.

She looked up at him, raising an eyebrow. "Being a bit presumptuous."

He chuckled. "You going to slap my face?"

"I'm thinking about it." But her eyelids had slid to half mast, and her eyes had turned sultry, her lips parting as her gaze rested on his mouth.

"Fair enough," he said. "I promise I won't kiss you unless you ask me to."

He meant it—if she wanted to take this any further, she was going to have to ask him. The last thing he wanted was to wake in the cold light of day and have Neve turn arctic on him again because he'd talked her into going to bed with him.

That didn't mean he couldn't try to convince her in other ways, though. He kept his gaze fixed on hers, and let thoughts filter through his mind about what he would do to her if she took him up to her room. Gone were the days when he'd strip her naked and have her on her back in less than ten seconds. If Neve succumbed, he'd want to take his time and make the most of having her in his arms.

He'd remove each item of clothing slowly, kissing her skin as he revealed it, until she stood before him in the sexy underwear he knew she'd be wearing beneath her clothes. He'd unclip her bra and draw it down her arms, feast his eyes on her generous breasts, and take his time to tease her soft nipples to buds with his teeth and tongue. Then he'd slide her panties down her thighs and let her step out of them, push her onto her back on the bed, and kiss up her thigh to her—

"Stop it," she said.

He blinked. "Stop what?"

"Picturing me naked. It's almost as if I can see your thoughts behind your eyes."

"Why? It's a harmless, fun pastime."

"Maybe you should try painting or gardening."

He chuckled and kissed her nose again. "So you're not picturing me naked then?"

"No." She moistened her lips.

"I wonder whether we're still as good together as we used to be." He thought back dreamily to the days where they'd barely gotten out of bed. Neve had been hungry for him and a willing guinea pig for anything he'd wanted to try. He hadn't believed his luck.

But it wasn't just what they'd done in bed that had been so great. It had been the way he felt about her. Pleasuring her had been like a drug he'd had to have over and over again, addicted to in the nicest possible way. Would it still be the same? Or had that been the passion of youth, something he'd outgrown over the years?

It didn't feel as if he'd outgrown her. Having her there, in his arms, it felt as if all the years had been stripped away. He had to fight not to let his hand drift down from her waist to her bottom, where he knew he'd want to tighten it on the soft muscle and pull her against him. His gaze roamed over her slightly parted lips, around to her pale neck, sliding down the V of her blouse that led temptingly to the curves beneath her sweater. He felt like he was twenty-one again, all hormones and hard-on, desperate to lose himself in her, to plunge into her softness and ride her until he found release. *Fucking hell.* What was wrong with him? Was he seducing her? Or was she bewitching him?

"Jesus," she said. "I feel like you're wearing x-ray specs. I feel naked."

He chuckled. "Sorry. It must seem very rude."

"Nobody's ever looked at me the way you do," she whispered.

"Bullshit," he scoffed. "You're gorgeous. You can't tell me that men don't look at you with desire."

"Not in the same way. They just want to get in my knickers."

"Yeah, well, I can't blame them for that."

"No, I mean… You've always looked at me as if…"

He tipped his head to the side, watching her lips move as she talked, imagining pressing his against them. "As if…"

"As if I'm covered in melted chocolate and you want to lick it all off."

"Now there's an idea."

Her lips curved up. "I seem to remember we tried that."

"I believe the sheets needed a wash afterward."

She giggled. "Yeah."

The song changed again, this time to another ballad that must have been on the radio a lot the year after they'd broken up, because it made him feel sad. Neve must have felt the same, because she turned her head and rested her cheek on his shoulder.

He didn't say anything, just slid his hand around to the small of her back, enjoying the feel of her against him. Her hair smelled of tropical fruit, mango maybe, and it mixed with the smell of brandy she'd been drinking. She'd taste sweet if he kissed her. Was she going to let him? He wasn't sure yet.

Over her shoulder, he looked up for the first time in a while and saw Lisa standing in the doorway to the bar, watching them. He smiled, and she smiled back, giving him a little wave before backing away and disappearing around the corner. She'd come to find him, maybe to ask if he wanted a drink, but she'd obviously realized there was something going on between him and Neve.

He rested his lips on Neve's hair. Was there something going on? He breathed her in, his senses swirling. It had been five years since they'd been together, and she'd been talking to him exactly one day— the feelings inside him couldn't be real. They had to be an echo of what he'd felt back then, a ripple through time. It was like having a memory of being a child and not knowing whether it was a real memory or if he'd seen a photograph of himself at that age.

All he knew was that he wanted her, and that having her in his arms made him happier than he'd felt in a long, long time.

Chapter Eleven

Rhett's hand was warm in Neve's, the other resting at the base of her spine, holding her against him.

He wasn't going to ask her to go to his room. She knew that now. He was so wary of her blaming him that he was going to wait for her to make the move.

She couldn't. After everything she'd been through, it would be a huge step back rather than the leap forward she'd been hoping to make while she was away.

And yet being with him felt so right. Why was that?

She wouldn't have been surprised to discover he used an aftershave with some kind of pheromone in it that reacted with her hormones. This close, she could feel her body preparing itself for him—her lips swelling and growing sensitive when she moistened them with her tongue, blood rushing to her nipples and between her legs, an ache between her thighs that wouldn't go away.

How could he make that happen just by dancing with her? She didn't know, and part of her resented him for having this effect on her. Did he know what he was doing? That he was seducing her, even though he wasn't exactly talking her into it?

Moving back a little, she lifted her head to look at him, to discuss it with him, but the words melted like snowflakes on her lips as she met his eyes. The way he looked at her wiped away any doubt or fear. It was as if he saw her as the huge chocolate sundae she'd been thinking about earlier. As if he wanted to eat her up.

Oh my...

Briefly, she thought about Scott, and about his wife, and wondered how he was doing in hospital. Life was so short, she thought. Was it better to regret the things she hadn't done, or the things she had?

She stopped moving. Rhett's eyebrows rose, his smile fading. "What?"

Saying nothing, she turned and retrieved her handbag, then started walking toward the door. After a few steps, she stopped and glanced over her shoulder. He was still standing by the table, staring at her.

She waited a moment. Her heart pounded so hard she almost felt herself moving with each thud.

Then she lifted a hand toward him.

He looked at it, then back up at her. He didn't smile, but the look in his eyes softened, like chocolate left in front of the fire. After picking up his jacket, he walked forward, took her hand, and followed her to the door.

They didn't speak while they waited for the elevator, nor while they rode it up to her floor, even though they were alone. They stood on opposite sides of the carriage, watching each other, Neve's heart thundering at the thought of what she was about to do. His eyes were thoughtful, and she wondered what he was thinking. Was he trying to decide whether they were doing the right thing? His gaze slid down her, and his lips curved up a little. He looked more like he was thinking about what he was going to do to her when he got her in the room.

Neve felt faint with anticipation and nerves. She'd invited a few guys back to her place over the years, but she'd never felt like this about a one-night stand before. Because that's what this would be, she reassured herself. She didn't have to worry about repercussions or what would happen afterward because this was all about sex, and really it was irrelevant that they'd once dated. But no one-night stand had ever looked at her like this. And her heart had never pounded so hard she felt as if she might pass out.

The carriage stopped, the doors dinged and opened, and she walked out with him, along the corridor to her room.

Her mouth had gone dry, and her mind was racing faster than her heart, which was saying something. What was she doing? Was she crazy? *Be sensible*, the angel on her left shoulder begged. *Think about how you'll feel in the morning.*

Pausing outside her door, she turned and waited until he stood before her. She studied the button on his shirt for a moment, then looked up at him. If there had been a fraction of a look of glee on his face, of smugness that he'd convinced her to do this, she would have said goodnight.

There wasn't, though. He was waiting patiently as if aware she needed to weigh this up before she made the final commitment. But there was no triumph there, or doubt. His lips were curved a little, and the only emotions his eyes held were affection, desire, and hope.

She swallowed hard. "Just this once, Rhett. Just physical. That's all this is, right?"

"Of course." His expression was unreadable.

Sliding her card out of her pocket, she inserted it in the lock and turned the handle. Then she took his hand and led him inside.

She'd left the heat pump on and the lights on the wall opposite the bed, so the room was warm and lit with a cozy glow. It was a basic room, but a nice one, with a queen bed, a table and chairs, and a small kitchenette with a sink, a kettle, and a microwave.

Walking in, she left her handbag on the counter and toed off her shoes, then placed them neatly beneath the chair.

Hearing water running, she straightened and saw that Rhett was in the process of filling the kettle, which he now plugged in and switched on.

"Thirsty?" she asked, amused and a little puzzled. He wanted a drink right now? She leaned against the wall, her hands tucked beneath her butt, not sure what to do. With other men, she might have taken the initiative, but all of a sudden she felt shy and unsure, not herself at all.

"A bit." He didn't elaborate. He took out his phone, selected something, then placed it in the speakers on the bedside table. Half of her expected him to have chosen a song that had been special to them while they'd been together, but instead sensual guitar playing filled the air, and then a guy started singing in a sexy soul voice about being at the edge of desire, sending skitters down her spine.

Rhett walked forward until he stood before her.

For a long moment, they just studied each other.

"I feel like a sixteen-year-old," she said, moistening her lips, her breasts rising and falling rapidly. Was he nervous too? He didn't look nervous. Instead, he moved a little closer to her, cupped her face with his hands, and lifted her chin so she looked into his eyes.

"Ask me," he murmured.

Tears pricked her eyes. Everything teetered on this moment. So far, she hadn't done anything she could regret, not really. Nothing she could blame herself for. If she went any further...

If only there was some kind of rulebook she could refer to at times like this. But there wasn't, there was only her own judgment, and she'd never been very confident of that.

His hands were warm on her face, and he brushed her bottom lip with his thumb, sending shivers skittering throughout her body.

"Ask me," he murmured again.

She was under his spell—there was no doubt about it. She couldn't look away from his eyes, entranced by the way they glowed green in the lamplight. They were hooded, fixed on hers. The softness had gone, and they were filled with a sexy desire.

"Ask me," he said a third time. Although he was giving her the option to turn him down, and he wouldn't do anything without her permission, his firm tone demanded she do as he said.

She swallowed. *Here I go, leaping off the cliff...* "Kiss me," she whispered.

His mouth curved up, and he exhaled with a long sigh of relief. Then he lowered his lips to hers.

Neve closed her eyes. She wasn't sure what she'd expected, but it wasn't this. On the whole, their lovemaking had been fast and furious, buttons popping, clothes flying, with little foreplay because she rarely needed it. She'd half expected them to walk into the room and for him to be inside her in seconds, thrusting them both to a climax before the kettle boiled.

But he didn't even kiss her properly, not to start with. He skated his lips across hers as if enjoying their softness, and continued to travel up her cheek, across her eyebrows, and down her nose before returning to her mouth. There he began pressing his lips to hers from one corner to the other, eventually returning to the middle, where she finally felt the touch of his tongue on her bottom lip.

She waited for him to turn the dial up to eleven and plunge his tongue into her mouth, but he seemed determined to confound her expectations, and instead teased her lips apart before sliding his tongue sensually against hers. He tasted of whisky, warm and exotic. Neve exhaled, feeling her breath mingling with his, all the hairs on her body standing on end at the sensation, and she tipped her head back on the wall, giving herself over to the kiss.

Mmm... She'd forgotten how good he was at this. He'd always seemed to know exactly what she wanted before she did, and this time he'd known how she needed to go slowly and be reminded what it could be like and how much she wanted him.

His hands had been cupping her face, and now he slid them further into her hair, the slight scrape of his fingers along her scalp forcing a small moan from her, and making her bring her hands up to rest on his chest.

His skin was warm through the crisp cotton shirt, and she splayed her fingers, feeling the muscles of his chest beneath it. He'd always had a fantastic physique, pushing himself to the peak of fitness. He'd eaten like a horse but had spent nearly all day every day in constant motion, and he'd been lean and wiry, with every muscle defined and toned to perfection. His lifestyle had changed now—had his body changed too? Suddenly she was desperate to find out.

Without even thinking, her fingers fumbled at the buttons of his shirt, but he didn't laugh or exclaim his victory. Instead, he murmured his approval and continued kissing her, apparently taking pleasure from caressing her lips and letting their tongues engage in the most sensual of dances.

Neve reached the last button and slid her hands up to the top to push the shirt over his shoulders. He dropped his hands momentarily to let it slip to the floor, lifting his head to look at her as she reached out to touch him.

She placed her fingers on his collarbone and stroked across to his shoulders, then over his pecs, brushing his nipples, and continuing down his abs. He'd filled out, and had lost the sinewy wiriness she remembered, but each muscle was still defined. He had the body of a man, not a youth, with an attractive scattering of manly hair across his chest tapering in an oh-so-happy trail that disappeared beneath the waistband of his trousers.

Returning her fingers to his arm, she traced around his tattoo. The secret mark, for her eyes only.

Looking up, she saw him watching her, smiling.

"Do you mind me looking?" she asked, trailing her fingers up his ribs.

He shook his head. "Have I changed?"

"You've grown up," she whispered. "Turned into a man."

He placed his hands on her hips, bending his head to kiss her again, still in a lazy, explorative way that continued to give her tingles all over, as if he was teasing pleasure from her a little at a time.

"Do I get to compare too?" he murmured, kissing around her cheek to her ear. He ran his tongue around it, and she shivered.

"If you want."

"I do want." He grasped hold of the base of her black sweater, and she lifted her arms so he could pull it over her head. He tossed it onto a nearby chair, then returned to undo the buttons of her blouse while he kissed her.

"I'd forgotten what it was like to take time over kissing," she murmured against his lips.

"You don't kiss the men you sleep with?" His lips still brushing hers, he unfastened the bottom button and parted the blouse.

Neve didn't reply, the question making her feel awkward. She didn't want to talk about other men she'd been with. It made her feel as if she'd been unfaithful, which was stupid because he'd been with other girls too. But it wasn't just that—it made her sad. She had kissed others, of course, but it hadn't been the same. It had always been about sex, and the fastest journey from A to B. And of course this was too—only Rhett wasn't kissing her as if that was his plan.

He removed her blouse and placed that on top of the sweater, and returned to examine what he'd revealed. "Aaahhh," he said, exhaling with satisfaction at the sight of her in a chocolate-brown lace bra. It was one of her favorites, from Rowan's Midnight in Paris collection, the lace of the cups covered in swirls that looked as if someone had drizzled melted chocolate all over her breasts. "Oh yeah."

"You approve?" she asked, somewhat wryly.

"Of course I approve. You look fucking amazing."

"Have I changed?"

He rested his hands on her hips again, then stroked up into the curve of her waist and up to the swell of her breasts. "You've grown up," he said, echoing her words. "Turned into a woman." He bent and touched his lips to her right shoulder, which bore a faint scar from where the wall had collapsed on her.

She felt shy at standing before him in her underwear—why did she feel shy? Normally she'd be stripping off everything to speed up the pace and get down to the good stuff. In many ways, it would have been less strange if they'd done that—fallen onto the bed in a tangle of limbs and tongues, maybe even had sex while clothed, getting carried away by passion.

But this felt... thought out. Planned. He hadn't gotten drunk and lost control. He knew perfectly well what he was doing. It reminded her of how skillful he'd been in the bedroom, and how he'd liked to take control of their lovemaking, something she'd not really let another man do since. It made her nervous.

"Shall we get into bed?" she asked in a small voice, wanting to speed things up so she didn't have time to think about whether she was doing the right thing.

His lips curved, and he moved closer to her, forcing her to back right up against the wall. "What's up, Neve? Having doubts?"

"N-no."

"You know you can stop me at any time." He ran his tongue along her bottom lip, then dipped it into her mouth before lifting his head again. "Do you want me to stop?" He nibbled her bottom lip. "You only have to say."

She didn't say anything, her mind spinning. She must have drunk too much brandy. Oddly though, her head felt clear, too clear—that was the problem. "I just thought we'd be... fast."

She'd thought he'd laugh at that—how come he was reacting so differently from what she'd expected? He slid his hands over her skin, making her nipples tighten in her bra without even touching them.

"Why would I want to go fast when I've been dreaming about this for years?" He kissed along her jaw to beneath her ear.

"Rhett..." She felt confused, not sure what she wanted, frightened of how much she ached for him, and scared of giving him power over her again.

He kissed back to her nose, then moved back. "I'm going to make a drink, and then I'm going to give you an orgasm that'll get rid of every bit of doubt you're having right now. So if you're not going to tell me to leave, take off your trousers, sit on the bed, and stop worrying."

Chapter Twelve

Neve's eyes widened, and her jaw dropped. She stared at Rhett, but he'd turned away and walked across to the kettle. He popped a teabag into a mug, added sugar, and poured in the hot water. Stirring it with a spoon, he glanced at her. When he saw her still standing there, he raised an eyebrow. "I'm waiting," he said softly.

She'd smothered her nerves at asking him up because she'd been certain he'd walk in, rip off her clothes, and take her hard and fast. It appeared that wasn't going to happen. Perhaps he was worried that next morning she would accuse him of not giving her enough time to think about what they were doing. If that was the case, he had a point. If left to her own devices, she was pretty sure she was going to talk herself out of it.

He removed the teabag, added a splash of milk, gave the mug a final stir, then walked back to her. Fixing his gaze on hers, he offered her the mug.

Neve caught her breath, memories flooding back. How could she have forgotten?

When they were together, he'd always taken charge in the bedroom. Initially, she'd let him because he'd been more experienced, but as time had passed and she'd grown more confident, she'd realized he wasn't just showing her the way—he enjoyed dominating her sexually. It wasn't about forcing her—although she'd pretended to fight him at times, they'd both understood the boundary between playful resistance and non-consensual. His technique was way more subtle.

But she'd forgotten about the significance of the tea. It had been a ritual he'd invented, a symbol of what he was expecting.

Often, when they'd been out for the evening and had arrived home together, she'd been as eager as he was to get into bed, and she'd stripped and then removed his clothing while pulling him toward the bedroom. Sometimes he'd let her, and occasionally he'd been the one to pick her up and carry her in, with the intention of finding the fastest way to the finishing line. She'd never needed a lot of foreplay, and quick and hard was sometimes just what the doctor ordered.

But sometimes, he'd gone into the kitchen and brewed a cup of tea, and had made her drink it with him, sip by sip, passing the mug backward and forward while he kissed her and murmured in her ear about what he was going to do to her when he eventually took her into the bedroom. It was his way of telling her he wanted to take it slow. The heat of the drink and its sweetness—even though she didn't usually take sugar—somehow served to ground and calm her. By the time they'd finished, she'd be simmering with a deep glow of desire, and she'd known they were in for a whole evening of lovemaking.

Automatically, she accepted the mug from him. The music changed to another song, some woman with a deep, sexy voice spiraling around her, singing about the pleasures of the body matching the pleasures of the mind, the slow, sultry beat making her want to swing her hips and dance.

She sipped the tea, and warmth flooded her mouth, heating her all the way down to her stomach. Did her body still remember what the taste meant? Did it carry within it an echo of the memory? She wasn't sure, but as she sipped it again and passed the mug back to him, looking into his eyes, she finally understood what he wanted her to do—to go at his pace, to follow his lead. Not only that—she understood that even though she pretended to herself that she didn't need him, and that she preferred her relationships to be on an equal footing, she'd missed this. The way he was with her—it turned her on. She longed for a man to tame her, and they both knew he was the one who could do it.

His gaze was still fixed on hers, and something was changing between them. Like the setting of the sun and the appearance of twilight, as she looked into his eyes, her breathing calmed and her panic died down. Just because he hadn't pushed her onto the bed and slipped inside her in seconds, it didn't mean this wasn't physical. He was just telling her that he knew what she needed—what they both needed—and they were going to take it slow.

Unhurriedly, she began to unbutton her trousers.

His lips curved up. Was she imagining it, or had relief lit his eyes? Perhaps he'd fully expected her to tell him to leave once she'd had a chance to think about what they were doing.

Well, she was past that now. After removing the trousers, she placed them over the chair. She wore a pair of panties and thigh highs that matched her bra, the elastic around the top of them embroidered with the same melted chocolate pattern as her underwear. Her body burned as his gaze slid down her, then returned to hers, his eyes a thousand degrees hotter. Jesus, how could he just look at her and make her melt?

Still keeping his gaze on hers, he placed the mug on the bedside table, took out his wallet, and placed it by his phone. Then he undid his belt and zipper and took off his trousers, laying them over the chair. After flicking off his socks, clad just in a pair of black boxer-briefs, he approached her again, cupped her face, and kissed her.

This time, he let the full heat of his passion sear through him, delving his tongue into her mouth. Neve moaned and slid her arms around him, stroking up his back. Ohhh… it was heavenly to touch and be touched like this. She loved the heat of his skin, the hardness of his muscles, the sexy scent of pure male wrapping around her and erasing everything else from her mind but the joy of being with him again.

Slipping his arms behind her, he held the catch of her bra between his fingers and pushed the clasps together.

Neve watched him move back as the elastic gave and the cups released her breasts, which returned to their natural shape, relaxing and softening. He drew the straps down her arms and tossed it onto the chair.

"Still so beautiful," he murmured, cupping her breasts. Following his gaze, she watched him brush his thumbs across the soft tips and saw the ends tighten into beads. Lowering his head, he covered one with his mouth and sucked gently, and Neve groaned, sinking her fingers into his hair. He swapped to the other one, teasing it with his tongue until it shone like the first, and a deep ache grew between her thighs.

Dropping to his haunches, he pulled her panties down her legs. She leaned on his shoulders and stepped out of them, and they joined the rest of their clothes.

He stood again and met her gaze. "Sit," he instructed.

She held her breath, her heart hammering. "No."

In reply, he pushed her, and she fell, laughing, back onto the mattress. Leaning across, he picked up the mug and took a large swig of tea, swirling it around his mouth as he sank onto his knees and pushed her thighs apart. Swallowing the tea, he immediately closed his hot mouth over her sensitive flesh.

Neve bucked and arched her back with a loud groan as she sank her hands into his hair. "Fuck... Rhett..." She'd never felt anything like it, and she almost came on the spot.

He slid his arms beneath her thighs, wrapped her legs around him, and proceeded to devote himself to fulfilling the promise he'd given to pleasure her.

God, how many months, years, had she dreamed about him doing this? He'd always been fantastic at oral sex, and he certainly hadn't lost his touch. He slid his tongue inside her, then replaced it with his fingers as he licked and sucked her folds and teased her clit with the tip of his tongue.

Keyed up through a whole evening of anticipation, within minutes she was panting and writhing beneath him. It only took a few more moments of stimulation before her muscles began to pulse, and she cried out and clenched her hands in his hair, riding the wave right up to the shore.

By the time he finally lifted his head, she was spent and exhausted. He surveyed her for a moment, then rose and placed soft kisses up her body until he leaned over and looked down at her.

Her eyes fluttered open, having trouble focusing on him. "Mmm," she said, closing them again. "Wow."

"You're so fucking sexy." He kissed up her neck before brushing his lips against hers.

"Yuck," she muttered, knowing that it wouldn't make him stop. When they'd first gotten together, she hadn't been a virgin but she'd been naive, and he'd taken great delight in doing his best to shock her and make her protest. Clearly, that hadn't changed.

He kissed her nose. "Move up the bed."

She flipped back the duvet and turned around on the bed to lie so her head was on the pillow. He slipped off his underwear and stretched out next to her, pulling her to face him so they lay on their sides. Lifting her chin, he kissed her, long and lingering, before finally moving back.

"Hey, beautiful," he said.

"Hey, handsome." She didn't mind saying it because it was true. He looked gorgeous lying there with his ruffled hair and glowing eyes.

"That was nice," he said. "Been dreaming about that for a long time."

He'd been thinking about having sex with her while they were apart? She didn't quite know what to say to that. Okay, she'd fantasized about him more than once over the last few years, but she would never have admitted that to him.

"Thanks for fulfilling your promise," she said.

He raised an eyebrow. "Oh, that wasn't the orgasm I was talking about."

"It wasn't?"

"Nuh-uh. That was just a warm up."

"I see." Her heart, which had been slowing down, began to pick up pace again. "So… we're not going to just roll over and go to sleep yet, then?"

He trailed his fingers lightly up her hip and ribs to her breast. "No." He drew a circle around her nipple, then took it between his finger and thumb and tugged it.

"Aaahhh…" Pleasure shot from her nipple to between her legs, faster than any speeding bullet.

Reaching across her, he picked up the mug of tea and took another big swallow, replaced the mug, then bent his mouth to her breast and closed it over the sensitive tip.

Neve groaned at the feeling of his hot tongue on the delicate skin. She was going to die from pleasure. The guy was going to sex her to death tonight, she was sure of it. Not that she was complaining. What a way to go…

He skimmed a hand down over her stomach and pushed her thighs apart. She obliged, sighing as he slid his fingers between her legs.

"Mmm," he murmured. "That's nice." He kissed her while he slipped his fingers inside her briefly before bringing them up to circle over her clit. "So swollen and wet. So ready for me."

She couldn't suppress a little shiver at his sultry tone. The years had done nothing to change the way he could manipulate her in bed. No matter how much she'd tried to rush things or to go at her own pace, he'd always been able to make her wait or speed her up, and his eyes told her he knew it.

A sliver of resentfulness slid down inside her. He would think she was at his beck and call again. Maybe he was laughing inside, smug that he'd crooked a finger and she'd come running. He'd known sex would be the thing to make her buckle.

Not wanting him to think he had complete control over her, she reared up, tipping him onto his back, and straddled him. In the past, he'd have fought her, determined to have the upper hand, but tonight he just laughed and held up his hands in a submissive gesture. "Ride me, cowgirl," he said. "I'm all yours."

Chapter Thirteen

Rhett stretched out beneath Neve, happy for her to think she was in control for a while.

She looked down at him, breathing heavily. Her dark bob had swung forward, her cheeks were flushed, and her eyes were wide with excitement. At least, he hoped it was excitement. When she'd tossed him onto his back, he thought he'd seen her eyes flash with resentment.

Leaning across him, she picked up his wallet and sat back, straddling his hips. Flicking open the wallet, she then took out the condom she'd obviously guessed was tucked inside.

"Just in case?" she said, tossing the wallet back onto the table.

He shrugged. It had been in there for about six months, but he wasn't going to admit that to her.

He'd slept with only a couple of girls since moving back to Wellington. He'd met them at nightclubs, and they'd both been mutual one-night stands. He wasn't ashamed to admit he'd wanted to make sure everything worked. He hadn't told them about his operation, and neither of them had noticed, or at least they hadn't commented on it if they had. But he hadn't been anywhere close to having a long-term relationship with anyone for years.

Mainly because he hadn't met anyone who matched up to Neve. But he wasn't going to tell her that either.

She looked down and studied the erection that jutted out between them. He felt a twinge of apprehension, remembering the resentment he thought he'd seen. She'd refused even to speak to him until that morning. This wasn't some huge revenge plan, was it? Would she pull out a pair of shears with a manic *Mwahaha!*?

She didn't, though. Instead, she locked her gaze on his and licked from the heel of her hand all the way up to her fingertips. Then she closed her hand around him and stroked up and down, dropping her gaze to admire her handiwork.

He groaned and closed his eyes, sinking his hands into his hair. How long had he dreamed about this? He swelled in her hand, and she murmured her approval, her fingers moving slickly over him. Jesus, that felt good. But he couldn't let her do it for long or he was going to come, and he had other things planned before he'd let that happen.

As if she'd read his mind, she stopped stroking him, and then he felt her fingers brush across the scar on his abdomen. He opened his eyes, his heart skipping a beat as he caught a look of tenderness and concern pass across her face. Although she had a heart of gold, she could be incredibly hard sometimes, and he'd never thought to see her look at him with affection again. Unexpected emotion washed over him, and it must have shown on his face, because she leaned forward to kiss him.

He closed his eyes again, enjoying the press of her breasts against his chest and the touch of her lips on his. Her tongue teased his lips apart, and he let her deepen the kiss, loving her slow exploration of him, her rediscovery.

Eventually, she pushed upright again, tore the wrapper off the condom, and carefully rolled it onto his erection. Then she shifted up a little, guided the tip of him underneath her, and moved until he parted her folds.

He rested his hands on her hips and looked into her eyes as he pushed up into her.

Both of them gave a long and happy sigh. Rhett felt everything around him begin to blur, almost as if time hadn't passed and he was back with her once again. It was a bit concerning because it suggested he'd drunk more than he'd thought and maybe he wasn't quite as in control as he'd hoped, but he didn't have time to think about it because Neve had started to move. She rocked her hips, forcing him to slide in and out of her, and it felt so blissful that everything else fled his mind.

"Mmm." She raised her hands and lifted her hair on top of her head, holding it there as she moved. She looked incredibly sexy atop him, naked except for her chocolate-patterned thigh highs. He knew she still went to the gym, and her body was toned and firm, her full breasts gleaming in the lamplight. He cupped them and tugged gently on her nipples, and she tipped back her head and moaned, still rocking.

He played with them for a while, and not surprisingly it wasn't long before her thrusts became more urgent. She ground against him with each movement of her hips, obviously arousing herself, judging by the way her breaths were becoming ragged.

"Nuh-uh," he stated. "Not yet." Sliding his arms around her, he held her tightly and flipped her onto her back.

She squealed. "Rhett!" Flopping back onto the pillow, she groaned. "I'd forgotten how you always stopped right when I was about to come, and how frustrating it was." Her chest heaved, and her face was flushed with passion.

Chuckling, holding the condom in place, he carefully withdrew. "Turn over," he demanded.

She met his gaze. Her blue eyes blazed. "No. And stop bossing me around."

He caught her arm and pulled it across her body, turning her onto her front, and then moved between her legs. She struggled, a little, but stopped as he slid a hand beneath her and stroked through her swollen folds.

"Come now," he murmured, maneuvering the tip of his erection to her opening. "You know I'm always right." Bracing himself on either side of her shoulders, he thrust forward.

"Oh!" She pulled down the pillow and buried her face in it. "Oh my God."

Rhett felt a glow of pleasure and a sense of everything settling into place as he sank deep into her. "Yes…" he hissed, bending to kiss her shoulder. "Oh yes, I've missed this. Haven't you missed it, Neve?"

"No." She clutched the pillow and groaned as he thrust. "Aaahhh…" Automatically, her thighs widened and she pushed back against him.

"Don't lie to me." He set up a steady pace, enjoying the position and the way he had her at his mercy. He'd always loved having her beneath him, spread wide for him. On her front, she could only lie there and let him proceed at his own pace. He liked that. "I know you love it like this. I know you love doing as you're told." He stifled a laugh, bending to nip her earlobe.

She shuddered. "Ahhh… I hate you. Oh…"

He kissed down her neck and slipped a hand beneath her to tug on her nipple. "Don't say that. You'll hurt my feelings."

She groaned, her fingers flexing on the pillow. Looking over her shoulder, she lifted a hand, caught a handful of his hair, and pulled his mouth down to hers.

"Ouch…" he grumbled. But he kissed her, plunging his tongue into her mouth, so turned on that his whole body felt like one big erogenous zone.

She released him and rested her forehead back on the pillow. "Oh…"

"Tell me you love this," he whispered, running a hand down her back and into the curve of her waist. He thrust harder, enjoying the sound of his hips meeting her butt. "Tell me you don't still love it rough."

"I… ah…" She braced a hand on the headboard so she could push back against him. "Never."

He moved his hand over her butt, caressed the silky skin, then slapped it.

She jumped. "Rhett!"

"Tell me."

"No."

He slowed his thrusts, doubt filtering through him. They'd always made love like this, with her half-protesting and fighting him all the way, but all of a sudden he didn't want it like that. He was wrong—time had passed, too much time, and he was no longer as sure of himself as he'd once been. Not where she was concerned, anyway.

Holding the condom, he withdrew again, causing her to give a long, heartfelt groan.

"For fuck's sake," she complained as he turned her onto her back, "I was about to come again. Orgasm deprivation isn't my favorite thing, just so you know."

"I'm sorry." He meant it this time.

She frowned. "What's the matter?"

He shook his head, moved his erection between her legs, and pushed into her. This time, though, he lowered down onto his elbows and kissed her as he began to thrust.

She took his face in her hands. "What's the matter? Did I hurt you?"

"No, no." He moved slowly inside her. "Kiss me."

She studied his face, then kissed him, long and lingering. "I was playing," she whispered when he finally lifted his head. "We always played like that, didn't we?"

"I know." He slipped a hand beneath her thigh and lifted it around his hips so he could sink deeper into her. "Not this time, though." He needed to see her face and know he wasn't reading the signs wrong.

Her frown softened, and she settled back onto the pillows, lifting her arms above her head. "I haven't changed, Rhett. I do still love the way you fuck me."

He knelt up, caught her hands in his, and held her there while he thrust. She was right—she hadn't changed.

But he had. And that was going to be a problem.

There would be time to think about that later. Right now, he was heading toward an orgasm at a rate of knots, and he wanted her there with him. Changing the angle, he ground against her while he thrust, and in less than a minute she was sinking her fingers into his hips, begging him, "Oh… Please… Don't stop, don't stop."

"I won't," he promised, and he rode her right through her orgasm, sighing as she clenched, her whole body tightening. She cried out his name, her muscles pulsing around him, and his throat tightened with emotion.

"Come on, baby," he said hoarsely, covering her mouth with his and capturing her final groans, and then his own climax swept him away and he lost himself in her. He was conscious of a feeling of bliss that wasn't just physical but born out of a sensation that, like a ship that had been rocking out of control, everything had righted and come to rest in the proper place, just for the briefest of moments.

He held onto it for as long as he could, but eventually it faded, and he opened his eyes and blinked to focus to see Neve's cool blue ones studying him, a smile on her lips.

"Hey." She kissed him. "You okay now?"

"I'm more than okay." He kissed her back, reveling in the afterglow, not wanting to let it go. He had to withdraw, though, and moved back with a groan. Discarding the condom, he fell back onto the pillows and held out an arm.

Neve looked down at it, and for a moment he thought she was going to refuse, but then she moved up close and rested her head on his shoulder.

"Mmm." He loved the feel of her pressed against him, soft and pliant. "You feel good."

"You too." She traced a finger down his chest and over his belly. "You were right."

"About what?"

"You can still get it up and ejaculate."

He laughed. "Yeah. Thank God."

"Does it feel different? Sex, I mean?"

"Nah. It's still terrific."

She chuckled. "We are good together, aren't we?"

"I think so. Did you enjoy it?"

She rested her chin on her hand. "Couldn't you tell?"

"You might have faked it."

"I'm not that good an actress."

They both smiled.

"Why did you stop?" she asked. "Before? What was the matter?"

"I… wanted to be sure you were enjoying it."

"Rhett, if I didn't want to have sex with you, you would have been aware, believe me. I'd have screamed the place down."

She'd meant to be funny, but it reminded him of the time he'd got it wrong before, when they'd had the big argument. He'd thought she was just playing then. It had been the worst mistake of his life.

"Yeah," he said. "I know. Even so."

She pressed her lips to his chest. "You're still bossy in bed."

"And you're still rebellious. Clearly, you need taming again."

Her eyes met his. He knew his question implied there might be a next time.

Just this once, Rhett. Just physical. That's all this is, right?

He couldn't think clearly—it was late, he'd had a lot to drink, and the after-sex hormones had flooded his system, making him sleepy. Neve yawned, apparently feeling the same.

"I should go," he murmured, reaching for his phone and turning off the music. He placed it back on the table and wrapped his arms around her.

"Yeah." She didn't move.

Rhett's lips curved up, and he closed his eyes.

Chapter Fourteen

Slowly, as if they were extremely heavy, Neve's eyelids fluttered open.

For a moment, she couldn't remember where she was. The windows were on the wrong side of the room, and it was oddly light—at home, her thick, dark curtains didn't let in an ounce of sunshine.

Then, gradually, as if her brain had been rebooted like a computer, memories started to filter through.

Her eyes widened, and her heart began to race.

She was lying on her side, but she rolled onto her back and placed a hand beside her.

The bed was empty.

Breathing fast, she got up and drew back the curtains, wincing as the sunlight sliced like sharp blades into her eyes. She walked over to the bathroom and pushed the door open gingerly, but she needn't have worried—that was empty too. He'd obviously left in the night without waking her.

Turning, she surveyed the room, images flickering through her mind like an old-fashioned movie reel. Rhett, letting his shirt slip to the floor… unbuttoning his trousers… pushing her onto the bed and burying his mouth in her… screwing her hard from behind… then turning her over and making love to her so tenderly it had almost made her cry.

Holy shit, what had she done?

Her head pounded, so she opened the tiny fridge and extracted a bottle of the water she'd left in there the night before and drank a good half of it. Then she found a couple of Panadol and took them with the other half of the water.

Wiping her mouth, she returned to the bed and sat on the edge. She'd slept all night without waking—something she hadn't done for a long, long time.

Leaning forward, she put her face in her hands. Holy Mary, Mother of God and all the saints, how much had she drunk the night before?

Oddly, she didn't remember it being that much. She'd had one glass of wine, then a few brandies, but it had been over several hours, and she'd drunk much more than that before with far less dire consequences. She'd not had any warning bells—the room hadn't spun, and she'd not noticed her speech or motion becoming impaired.

She sank her hands into her hair. The truth was that she hadn't been drunk—or at least, not so much that she could blame all of what she'd done on alcohol. It might have peeled off her safety labels, but it hadn't made her do anything she hadn't wanted to do deep down. The reasons could be debated—she'd been upset by what had happened to Scott and shaken by Rhett's admission that he'd had cancer, and he'd been charming and attentive, which was just what her lonely self had needed. She couldn't blame any of those on the Cognac.

Even so… how could she have been so stupid?

She looked to the side at where he'd been lying. A shiver ran down her spine at the memory of how she'd sat astride him and welcomed him inside her. At the time, it had felt like it was exactly where she should be at that moment—as if all the jigsaw pieces had slotted into place and finally made a complete picture.

Now she felt bemused as to why she would have thought it would be anything but idiotic to have sex with him. She'd spent years hiding her hurt behind a wall of anger and resentment—her fury had been the only thing that had stopped her dissolving into despondency. He'd treated her abysmally at the time, and what they'd done last night hadn't put any of that right. If he thought it had, he was going to be sorely mistaken.

He'd obviously left in the early hours. Why had he chosen to leave? And why hadn't he woken her?

She flopped back onto the bed and pushed the heels of her hands into her eyes. She was the most stupid woman who had ever lived.

Maybe the worst thing, though, was that although she knew she'd been dumb, she couldn't bring herself to regret it.

Did he regret it? Was that why he'd left? He'd been drinking whisky, and although like her he hadn't seemed anywhere near drunk, it would still have affected him, maybe more than he'd anticipated. Presumably he'd roused, realized what they'd done, and thought it would be easier to return to his room than to face her in the morning.

Emotion washed over her, and she took a deep breath and clenched her jaw hard, fighting against tears. She forced herself to blow out a long, slow breath. Okay, okay, it wasn't the end of the world. They were two grown, consenting adults, and all they'd done was have sex. She should focus on that and stop acting as if it changed everything. There was nothing wrong with having the occasional one-night stand. The fact that they'd once dated—and that he'd broken her heart—was irrelevant. They'd had sex—correction, they'd had great sex—and there was nothing wrong with that, as long as both of them accepted it didn't change the past, and they agreed they wouldn't let it affect the future.

Was he thinking the same thing at the moment? She was woman enough to hope he didn't regret it. He'd seemed to enjoy himself. She thought about how he'd turned her forcefully onto her front and taken her hard. She'd always loved him doing that, and she shivered to think of his strong hands and the way he used his weight and strength to pin her down.

But then he'd stopped and brought her back to face him, worried, so he'd said, that it wasn't what she'd wanted. That hadn't been the old Rhett talking. There had been tenderness in his eyes she'd never seen before. When he was young, he'd been affectionate, but never tender. It wasn't until now that she realized that.

She stretched out a hand and rested it on the pillow, then sat up in surprise as her fingers found a piece of paper. It was white—the same color as the pillow, a piece of hotel stationery, folded in half and carefully torn into a shape. Her lips parted in surprise as she opened it to reveal a heart. He hadn't written anything, but he'd left her a heart on her pillow.

She covered her mouth with a hand and studied it. What did it mean? He was a guy, so it might not mean anything, but then again it must mean something or he wouldn't have bothered leaving it at all. Was he just saying thank you, and making the point that he hadn't left for any reason other than because he needed to go back to his room to shower and get ready for the day?

Or did it mean something more?

She put it aside and checked the clock on the bedside table. Nearly seven thirty—she'd slept in. Must have been all the exercise, she thought, and stifled a hysterical urge to laugh. She just had time for a shower before breakfast. There was no point in worrying about what was done. She had to think about what happened next.

While she showered and dressed, she tried to work out how she felt about what she'd done, and how she should react when she saw him. She kept going around in circles, though, and eventually, when she'd shampooed her hair for the third time while she daydreamed about how he'd looked into her eyes while he moved inside her, she decided she wasn't going to think about it anymore.

After she'd dried herself, as she dressed, she told herself that she'd play it by ear when she saw him. Basically, it had been a one-night stand they'd both wanted to happen. Neither of them had been cajoled into it—he'd made sure of that when he'd cupped her face and said, "Ask me," before he kissed her.

Her hands paused in the process of doing up a button on her black shirt as she remembered the way he'd pressed his lips to hers so gently.

Then she carried on.

After blow-drying her hair, she pinned the ends up with a silver clip, hoping it made her look more professional, and had one last glance in the mirror. Would anyone be able to tell what had happened the night before? Would Lisa or any of the others have guessed—or maybe even seen them?

She set her jaw. So what if they had? It was nobody else's business.

Her head throbbed. Jeez. She needed a glass of orange juice the size of a swimming pool.

She made her way down to the restaurant with a racing heart, her mind drifting back to the last time she'd felt like this. On the day of Willow and Liam's wedding, Rhett had been unable to take his eyes off her. He'd flirted with her all day and danced with her all night. She'd had stars in her eyes, and when he'd casually suggested she go back to his hotel room with him, she'd said yes without a second thought. The next morning, they'd gone down to breakfast with the others, denying the accusations but their huge grins telling everyone the truth.

This was different, though. For a start, he hadn't stayed the night, and she had no idea what reaction he was going to have. Would he mention it? She didn't know whether she wanted him to or not. She didn't want him to act as if that one night had wiped away all their problems, but equally she couldn't deny to herself that she hoped he wouldn't just pretend it hadn't happened.

Pausing at the entrance to the restaurant, she glanced around. She spotted him instantly, sitting at a large table with several others she recognized from the course. Today, he wore a navy suit with a light blue shirt and a blue-and-gray tie. His jacket hung over the chair, and he wore a sexy gray sweater over the shirt.

Neve hesitated. Part of her wanted to choose an empty table and avoid the issue, but she knew it might seem rude when she'd spoken to some of the other attendees the day before. Besides which, she had to remember why she was here—for her business, to learn and make connections.

Taking a deep breath, she walked across to the half-filled table, chose a seat a few down from Rhett, and sat.

"Morning." She smiled at the people around her, accepting a glass of orange juice from the woman opposite who poured it for her. Then the waitress came up and asked what she'd like for breakfast, and she ordered muesli with fresh fruit and coffee. She spread her serviette across her knees, drank half her orange juice, and chatted to the man on her left about the workshops the day before.

Then, finally, she let her gaze slide across to Rhett.

He was watching her, leaning back in his chair, his fingers resting on his lips. She couldn't see if he was smiling. His eyes met hers, though, and in spite of her insistence that it didn't matter if he ignored her, she was relieved when he held her gaze and his eyes were warm. Then he winked at her.

Neve looked down and rearranged her cutlery. Her face burned. How did he manage to make her feel like a fifteen-year-old bashful virgin?

She didn't look up at him again, spending the next half an hour or so eating her breakfast and listening to the conversation around her. The other conference attendees were confident and knowledgeable about their businesses, and she felt a twinge of shame at the way she'd thought everyone would drone on and bore her. She really should learn not to make judgments like that.

Nobody mentioned the fact that she'd spent the previous evening with Rhett, not even Lisa, who joined the table shortly after Neve. Gradually, she began to relax. It hadn't been a huge mistake. It had been a lovely treat when she'd been feeling down—a way to reconnect with a man she liked, without dragging in their past.

She finished her breakfast and coffee, beginning to feel a little more normal, and decided to return to her room to collect her laptop and other items ready for the morning session. Trying not to look at Rhett, she tucked her chair under the table, left the restaurant, and walked across the foyer.

"Neve."

She glanced over her shoulder to see him a few steps behind her. Her mouth going dry, she stopped and turned to face him.

"Morning," she said.

He paused in front of her. To anyone watching, he would have seemed a decent distance away, she thought, hardly invading her personal space, and yet her body tingled as if he'd pushed her up against a wall and touched his lips to her cheek.

"Morning." He said nothing else, just met her gaze, and they looked into each other's eyes for a long moment.

Neve found herself tongue-tied—something that hadn't happened for a very long time, almost unable to breathe at the warmth and affection evident in his expression. Heat flooded her again as she thought about what they'd done the night before. It was just sex, she thought desperately. It didn't mean anything. But his eyes said that it did, and she couldn't look away.

He tipped his head to the side and smiled. "Why Miss Clark, you're blushing."

"I am not."

He chuckled. "It suits you. You're very pale normally."

That probably was true. Over the summer she hadn't ventured out much, and her skin hadn't captured the usual rosy glow it normally bore at that time of year.

"Thank you," he said softly.

She couldn't say anything glib to that. "Thank *you*," she repeated. "It was nice."

"I'm sorry I left but you said you'd had trouble sleeping, and it seemed a shame to wake you."

"It's okay, I don't mind. I just thought…" She stopped.

"Thought what?"

"That maybe you regretted it."

His gaze fell to her lips. "I don't regret it. Do you?"

Automatically, she moistened them with the tip of her tongue. "No."

He studied her mouth for a long moment, as if remembering kissing her, or thinking about kissing her again. Then his gaze rose to meet hers. "Good."

She swallowed hard. She had to say something or she was going to drown in his eyes. "I enjoyed it. And I'm glad that we're talking again. But it was just a one-night stand. A one-off."

"Of course," he said, still looking at her in a way that made her think he was imagining peeling off her clothes.

"It was purely a thing of the moment," she clarified. "It didn't resolve anything, Rhett. I have to make that point."

His smile faded a little, and he looked down at his shoes for a long moment. Then he looked up and smiled. "Sure." He was holding his jacket, and now he pulled it on and did up the front buttons. "No worries." He tugged down the cuffs of his shirt sleeves with the peculiarly masculine gesture that men did. "Hope you enjoy the morning's workshops. I'll catch you later."

"Yeah, see you." She watched him walk away toward the conference room. He looked every inch the businessman, and in many ways he'd changed so much. However, the cufflinks that had peeped out of his jacket had reminded her that inside he was still the man she'd fallen in love with. They were tiny shuttlecocks, ones she'd bought him all those years ago. Had he chosen them on purpose? And if he had, why?

Chewing on her bottom lip, she headed for the elevator, determined to put him out of her mind and concentrate on business for the rest of the day.

Chapter Fifteen

For the rest of the morning, Rhett attempted to dismiss the melancholy that threatened to swamp him and threw himself into the morning's proceedings. Due to his extensive knowledge of Facebook advertising, he was running the Facebook workshops. He turned his chair away from the rest of the room and spent an hour and a half talking intently to the people at his table, answering questions and sorting out any issues that arose.

Neve had joined the Twitter group, but he made sure he didn't go anywhere near her and let her be. Although she'd said she didn't regret what had happened the previous night, he wasn't so sure. She'd been keen to make it clear that it had been a one-off—a fact that disappointed him more than he'd expected.

As the session wore on, he scolded himself mentally for daring to think having sex with her might have meant something. What had he expected? That she would fall into his arms and declare she'd finally moved on? He'd wondered whether, if and when he finally got her to talk to him, he'd be able to convince her to put the past behind them and start afresh. Now, though, he realized how stupid he'd been. He would never be able to start afresh with her. It was like planting new seeds in the spring—it might seem as if last year's plants had died, but all they'd done was decay and mulch into the earth, and a detailed examination of the soil would show they hadn't magically vanished.

It made him sad, because although at the time he'd been so angry that he'd never wanted to see her again, after his illness he seemed to have lost all the fury that had driven him through his youth, and he'd wanted nothing more than to be on speaking terms with her again. He hadn't planned for it to go further than that. He'd thought he'd be happy just being friends.

When he'd visited London, a cabbie had told him how the River Fleet still ran beneath the pavements and roads, hidden by the modern-day city. This morning, he finally understood that his feelings for Neve were the same, flowing beneath the surface even though he thought he'd paved over them. Sleeping with her had been a bad idea. She would never let the past go, and all he'd done was make himself frustrated that he hadn't learned his lesson.

Trying not to think about it, he had morning coffee with Lisa and couple of the other organizers, then returned to his table for the second session. To his surprise, Neve was already there, tapping away on her laptop. He smiled at her, and she gave a small smile in return. No doubt she was desperate to discover about Facebook advertising and had decided to put aside her personal feelings for the sake of her business.

However, as he welcomed the other attendees to the table, he felt her gaze lingering on him. She sucked on the end of her pen as she leaned back in her chair, and his one-track mind had trouble steering away from picturing her lips closing around the tip of his erection as she knelt before him.

For fuck's sake. He scolded himself as he stood and welcomed everyone to the table. *Focus, Taylor.*

For a while it worked, and he lost himself in explaining the mechanics behind the social networking platform, giving examples of adverts that had worked, as well as ones that hadn't. He talked about how businesses had to make sure any photos they used with the ad didn't have more than twenty percent text on them, and the kind of pictures that worked the best. Then he talked about the sort of photos that couldn't be used, such as those promoting the use of drugs, tobacco, or weapons, or any that included adult content, including excessive amounts of skin or cleavage.

"That might be a problem for me," Neve said. "I sell lingerie and swimwear," she explained to the others around the table. "How do I get around the problem of not showing skin and cleavage?" She turned her cool blue eyes up to him.

Rhett met her gaze, hesitating for a moment, uncertain whether she'd meant to conjure up pictures of herself in her melted-chocolate underwear from the night before in his mind. Her gaze looked innocent, though, and it was a sensible enough question.

Trying not to think about what bra and panties she was wearing beneath her black shirt and gray pants, he cleared his throat. "That's a good question. Any ideas, anyone?"

"You could lay the swimwear out on a rock by the beach," someone suggested.

"Yeah, and put the lingerie on a bed," another woman said. "With candles around it. Make the photo suggestive without being revealing, you know?"

Neve nodded and tapped into her laptop. "That's a great idea."

"I think that's a very good point," Rhett added. "There are lots of ways you could be suggestive without showing anything."

She glanced up at him. Her lips curved up. "Right."

A couple of the others chuckled.

He grinned. "I'm serious."

She rolled her eyes. "You mean, like, have a couple of melons in the photo?"

That made them all laugh. "Not quite," he said wryly. He walked around to her and gestured at her laptop. "May I?"

She leaned back. "Sure."

"There are several stock photo sites you can use if you don't want to pay for a private photoshoot." He named one and waited for everyone to find the website. "Now, put in some words related to your product and check out the kinds of pictures it suggests." He tapped the word hourglass into Neve's laptop and pressed Go. "You could have some symbolic objects, like an hourglass, for example, because your brand targets the fuller or more rounded figure." He showed her some of the photos on the site. "Another way to go would be to have a photoshoot done using mannequins to model the lingerie like you did for your Valentine's Day shop display, and concentrate on the Four Seasons brand backed with colors of the seasons or, for example, the Eiffel Tower at night for the Midnight in Paris collection."

He was leaning quite close to her now, and he could smell the mint shampoo she'd used for her hair. When she looked up at him, it was easy to see the surprise in her eyes.

"How did you know the lingerie I wore last night was from that collection?" she whispered, glancing around to make sure nobody could hear her.

"Oh, studying ladies' underwear is a hobby of mine," he said softly, his gaze dropping to her mouth. Then he frowned. "Actually, scratch that. It sounds kinda creepy."

She chuckled. "Come on, tell me."

"Callie showed me the new Four Seasons' brochure a few weeks ago." He'd admired the Midnight in Paris collection then—he hadn't thought to see it modelled personally.

"Ah. That makes more sense." She moistened her lips. "Don't look at me like that."

"Like what?"

"Like you're thinking about me naked."

"I'm not. I'm thinking about you in sexy lingerie. Is that allowed?"

Her lips twitched. "No."

"Aw. You're no fun."

"I mean it, Rhett. Last night was… lovely, but it was a one-off." Her words said one thing—her eyes said another. Her eyes said she wanted him, and it made his heart leap.

"Sure," he said easily. "I know that. Doesn't mean we can't have a little fun now we're friends though, right?"

She cleared her throat. "Fun?"

He gestured around the table. "Talking, chatting with colleagues." He looked back at her, and he could tell by the wry twist to her lips that she knew he was teasing.

"Yes. It was nice to 'talk' again," she murmured, putting air quotes around the word.

"Good." He so wanted to kiss her. He knew her lips would be soft, and they'd part willingly to allow him to slip his tongue into her mouth. She'd taste of the extra-strong mints sitting by her laptop that she'd popped for years. Since they'd broken up, he hadn't been able to have one without thinking of her.

But they were surrounded by people, some of whom were casting them amused looks, obviously picking up on the attraction between them, so he stood reluctantly and walked around the table to see if anyone else needed any help.

It seemed like no time at all until the session had finished and Lisa was taking the podium to address them all.

"It's time to head off to Sky Peak," she announced. "You'll have a couple of hours either to try the ski slopes or the snowboarding slopes, to walk one of the beautiful trails, or just to sit and enjoy the magnificent scenery while you have lunch. Then for those of you who booked we'll move onto the Sky Peak Distillery for a tour and a tasting of their traditional vodka, their single malt whisky, and their delicious liqueurs. But this isn't just for pleasure! We'll return to the hotel for dinner, and then we'll have an after-dinner talk by John Lyttleton, one of the top marketing experts in the country, who'll draw on examples from the ski resort and distillery, so make sure you keep your eyes open!" She smiled. "Please meet out the front by the buses at twelve thirty sharp."

Rhett packed up his laptop and tucked it under his arm. He looked up to see Neve watching him. When she saw him look at her, she came around the table to stand before him.

"I'd lay all my savings on the fact that you're going to try out the snowboarding slopes," she teased.

He grinned. "Yep. You?"

"Wouldn't miss it for the world." Her cheeks were flushed, her eyes bright. She looked better than she had when he'd first seen her, pale and tired with lines drawn around her mouth that had spoken of pain—maybe not physical, but pain nevertheless. "Are you going to the distillery afterward?" she asked.

"Wouldn't miss it for the world."

They both laughed.

"Okay." She shouldered her laptop bag. "I'll meet you out the front?"

"Sure." He watched her walk away, his heart racing. *Don't get carried away*, he scolded himself. She was just enjoying the fact that they were talking again—there was no way she would be interested in anything more.

Still, he had a smile on his face as he returned to his room, and it wouldn't go away no matter how much he tried to make it.

*

They sat together on the coach to Sky Peak, a journey of about fifty minutes that wasn't long enough, Rhett thought, because he was enjoying himself so much.

For a start, the scenery was amazing. The road skirted the edges of the Southern Alps, gradually climbing toward the snow-topped peaks. The slopes were painted myriad shades of green and brown, broken up by dark evergreen forests and scattered with thousands of sheep. As the road rose, it started to snow and therefore the temperature must have dropped, but inside the coach it was warm and bright, and everyone was in high spirits.

Neve was at her best—cheerful and light-hearted. Although she carefully steered the conversation away from anything personal, her tone was mildly flirtatious, as if—for the duration of the conference at least—she'd put aside the problems of the past and was concentrating on just being with him.

She told him some funny stories about her lingerie parties—for example the time when the husband of the woman hosting the party came home early and was so intrigued by the items in Neve's basket of toys that he bought the whole lot, prompting his wife to turn completely scarlet in front of her friends.

"I couldn't keep a straight face," Neve said. "The poor woman was so embarrassed."

Rhett smiled. "I think it's great that you encourage women to step outside their comfort zones. Does it ever happen that their husbands or partners resent them bringing home their purchases?"

She studied him thoughtfully, her blue eyes the color of the snow-filled sky. "Well, I'd never know if that were the case, but I'm guessing that's very rare. Obviously, there are some men who are uncomfortable with the idea of using sexy lingerie or toys because they're embarrassed or feel threatened or whatever, but from what I've gathered it's usually the women who are holding back. To be honest, though, the sort of women who aren't interested in experimenting aren't my target audience, and they probably wouldn't come to our parties anyway, because I state quite clearly to the host what I'll be bringing so there are no shocked faces when I produce the case."

"So who is your target audience?" he asked, as much because he loved hearing her voice as because he wanted to find out.

"Firstly, those women who are already using lingerie and toys, because they'll encourage those who aren't but would secretly like to. Really, anyone who's open minded. Lots of women are too worried to go online and shop in case their kids or someone else opens any deliveries, and they don't want any rude names on their credit card bills. Having Four Seasons means nothing to the untrained eye, and every girl needs underwear."

"They do indeed," he agreed. "Have you thought about holding parties for men?"

Her eyebrows rose. "Seriously?"

"Why not? Maybe they'd buy for their partners—it's difficult for guys to buy stuff too, for the same reasons."

"Not sure I'd be comfortable talking about sex toys with a group of guys."

He snorted. "You'd have no trouble. You can make a man feel an inch high with one stab of those eyes. But I get your point. What about advertising for a fun addition to a dinner party instead? Couples could shop together then and egg each other on."

"I hadn't thought of that."

"There you go. I'm full of bright ideas. Speaking of which…" He decided to make the most of her mischievous mood. "I'm guessing you haven't had a chance to try out your new toy?"

Her lips curved up. "No, not yet."

"It makes sense to me that you practice all of its abilities, so you can talk about it with authority."

"Meaning…"

"If you need someone to help you test the remote control, I'd be happy to volunteer."

"I bet you would." She caught and held his gaze. Her smile faded a little. "I'm not sure that would be a good idea," she whispered.

"It would be purely for research," he said. "I wouldn't be getting any pleasure from it." His gaze rested on her mouth. "You would, though, hopefully."

She swallowed. "Why does the idea of controlling me turn you on so much?"

He shrugged. "Tell me that the notion of being at my mercy doesn't turn you on."

Her lips parted, but obviously she couldn't bring herself to voice the lie.

"Yeah," he murmured. "Thought as much."

"You're not the boss of me."

"If you say so." He smiled. She was right. The thought of being in charge of her arousal from a distance made his blood heat to boiling point, and the longing in her eyes told him she felt the same.

She looked away, out of the window. He could see her pulse racing in her throat. Leaning back in his seat, he let a small smile play on his lips. If she was able to relinquish full control to him, it would bode very well for the future.

Because although Neve had decided that last night had been a one-off, Rhett had very different ideas.

Chapter Sixteen

Neve hadn't been skiing for a long time, and Sky Peaks was an amazing alpine resort, with three terrain parks that catered for beginners through to advanced skiers, and all sorts of programs for teaching kids from toddlers to teens. It also had a variety of parks and pipes for snowboarders with jumps and jibs for all abilities, and featured a twenty-two foot superpipe, the largest in New Zealand, and an eighty-five foot table for the pros.

She knew Rhett would be itching to get out there, and she was looking forward to it too. She'd have to make sure she stayed on the beginner park, though, because her concentration had been shot since Rhett had looked into her eyes and told her he wanted to try out the remote-controlled vibrator.

She wasn't going to let him do it, of course. Sleeping with him once had been a terrible lapse, but she could put that down to alcohol and being lonely and wanting to show him how pleased she was that he'd gotten over his illness. But to do so again... She wouldn't be able to put that down to anything except good, old-fashioned lust. On its own, lust wasn't a problem, and in fact the idea of a steamy fling with him while they were away was most appealing. But although it felt as if this break in Queenstown was like a beautiful flower she'd discovered in the snow, Neve knew she shouldn't fool herself. The roots of the flower went deep into their past, and she couldn't pick the flower without pulling out a whole heap of things she'd rather leave buried.

So she tried to put Rhett's sexy suggestion to the back of her mind and followed him into the resort, where they hired jackets and pants, helmets, and wrist guards. They changed in the dressing rooms before picking up their snowboards and heading out to the chairlift.

Mounting the chairlift was a challenge with the snowboard attached to one foot, but Neve watched the couple in front of them and followed their lead, and in seconds they were spirited away to a silent, frozen world of stupendous beauty. It was snowing lightly, and it felt as if the whole world was holding its breath.

"Jesus." Rhett lowered the safety bar, staring at the view. "This place is amazing."

Her breath misted before her face. "I feel like I'm at the North Pole. I expect to see Santa riding past on Rudolph."

Neve had holidayed in Europe with her family when she was younger. They'd traveled to some of the major cities, gone skiing in the Alps, and spent Christmas with distant family in England. It had been odd to pass the festive season in the cold, and equally she could see why people from the northern hemisphere got so mixed up when they travelled to the south. In New Zealand, they still celebrated Christmas in December and cards bore snow and robins and all the traditional wintry symbols, and yet it was early summer, with Christmas Day often spent either at the beach or around the pool, if you were lucky enough to have one.

Conversely, at the solstice in mid-June, celebrations were carried out at Stonehenge in England to mark the longest day, but it was the shortest day Down Under, and it indicated the onset of winter. It was also the festival of Matariki—the Maori New Year—and in June many Kiwi families decorated their houses with festive lights or trees and exchanged presents, either to mark Matariki or in celebration of the ancient festival of Yule as a wistful nod to their European backgrounds.

Back at the hotel, there would be a party on the last night of the conference with a traditional roast dinner to mark the day. It was all very normal for Kiwis, and it seemed perfectly natural to Neve to picture Santa riding on his sleigh through the snow in June.

Rhett laid his arm along the back of the seat, caught her shoulder, and pulled her tight against him. "To keep you safe," he explained. "Don't want you to fall off."

"Yeah, right." She scoffed, but her heart had picked up speed at being close to him, even if they were separated by thick jackets and several other layers. He'd lifted his goggles on top of his woolly hat, and his hazel eyes were mainly green today, telling her he was excited to be out in the snow.

"Your eyes are the color of the sky here," he said softly.

She lowered her gaze for a moment, unnerved by his seriousness. "Men always say my eyes are cold," she said, a little wistfully. She knew she was sharp at times because stupidity and ignorance irritated her, but she would never have called herself cold.

"Clearly they don't know you very well then."

She looked up again, and he was smiling. "You don't think I'm cold?" She knew she sounded a tad pathetic but was unable to keep the hope out of her voice.

He chuckled. "Opposite end of the spectrum, sweetheart. Volcanic, is how I think of you."

She studied him, automatically wanting to distrust the compliment, to search for an ulterior motive, but in his eyes she saw only genuine affection and warmth.

"Don't look like that," he murmured.

"Like what?"

"Wary. It makes me sad."

"It's kind of my default setting nowadays."

"It shouldn't be, and I'm sorry if I had any part in it."

She looked down at her hands, and because she didn't know what to say, and because he looked as if he wanted to kiss her, she fished out her colored lip balm and applied some, pressing her lips together.

"Is that supposed to be a deterrent?" he asked, amused.

"Yes."

"Didn't work." He slipped a hand to the back of her head and leaned across to kiss her.

In spite of the cold, Neve's cheeks heated as his lips moved across hers, slow and sensual, claiming what he wanted from her. She should protest—she should push him away and declare her outrage.

She didn't though. Instead, she gave a little sigh and accepted it, closing her eyes and letting the peace, the silence, and the touch of his lips calm her and soothe her. Snow fluttered down on them, but it only added to the wintry magic.

When he lifted his head, his lips were fluorescent pink, the same as hers. He smacked them together. "What do you think?"

"Classy."

"Tastes nice," he said, running a tongue over them.

She shivered. "Don't." Her nipples tightened in her bra, and she felt an answering clench deep inside at the memory of what he'd done with that tongue.

"Given any thought to the remote control?" Mischievousness lit his expression.

"No."

"Liar." That one word, said in his deep voice and accompanied by the curve of his lips, got her right in the stomach.

"Rhett…" She couldn't think how to voice her desperation, but he just laughed and lifted the safety bar.

With shock, she realized their chairlift had arrived and it was time to disembark. "Shit. How do we get off this thing?" Her left boot was strapped in but the right still hung free.

"Wait until the lift slows down," he instructed, turning in the seat to show her. "As the board touches the snow, use the stomp pad for the back foot."

She did so, felt the pad grip her boot, and followed his lead as he pushed up onto his feet. The natural slope led them away from the chairlift, where they scooted to a slow stop a few feet away.

"Easy as," he said. Excitement ran through him like electricity. She wasn't sure if it was from the kiss or the anticipation of getting out on the snow. Maybe both.

They headed first for the training slopes, as Neve had only been snowboarding once before. Rhett led her through the mellow jumps and the handful of ride-on jib features. Blessed with naturally good balance, it wasn't long before she found her feet and her confidence grew, and soon the two of them switched to an intermediate lane, moving faster along the numerous features.

She'd reached her limit though, and she could tell he was itching to move on, so she sent him on his way and, after another thirty minutes or so, made her way to the viewers' gallery at the top of the Zero G advanced park. The fast-flowing trail featured sweepers, rollers, jumps, berms, and road gaps, and it wasn't long before she spotted him in his bright blue jacket and red pants, jibbing and freestyle boarding like a pro.

She hadn't realized he was so expert at it, and she shook her head with wonder. When they were together, she'd often watched him training at parkour, developing his balance and flexibility. He'd fascinated her with the way he'd seemed to defy gravity, and it was no different watching him snowboarding. How did he have such confidence in his body? She hardly considered herself old, but she knew she'd lost some of her youthful suppleness. Rhett played like a fifteen-year-old, fast and furious. Clearly, he'd worked hard to make sure his operation had had little to no effect on his fitness.

At the thought of his operation, her breath caught in her throat. Another twist of events, a different path in time, and he might not be here now, full of life, the sheer force of nature that filled her heart with joy in spite of their past. How would she have felt if things had turned out the other way? If one evening while at the bar with their friends, Liam had announced that Rhett had died?

Her brain couldn't comprehend the enormity of that possibility. He was too young, too gorgeous, too... alive. How could he have been so sick? How could he have had cancer, for Christ's sake? It didn't make sense. She got a pain in the chest when she thought about what might have happened, when she thought of him lying in a hospital bed, pale and weak, breathing his last breath...

Stop it, stop it, stop it. Hot tears coursed down her cheeks, and she had to walk away from the other people watching to hide her face. It was stupid to think like that. He wasn't sick—look at him, for crying out loud! He was currently twisting in the air, spinning around as he flipped up off a snow-covered wall, and finishing with a complete somersault before landing easily on his feet. He couldn't have been more alive.

Taking deep breaths, she tried to console herself. It was normal to feel this way if you thought about your friends being sick. She would have felt the same if Callie, or Birdie, or Liam had been diagnosed with cancer. It was just the distress of thinking about young life coming to a sudden end and making her think of her own mortality.

The softly falling snow fell on her hot cheeks, calming her, and as it settled she felt shame settle along with it. She'd always tried not to lie, and right now she was telling herself a whopper. Knowing he'd been sick—that he'd had cancer—was a shock the like of which she'd never experienced before, and it wasn't just because he was a friend. She'd loved him, and although they'd broken up, she'd assumed he'd always be around, somewhere, probably meeting other women, settling down, having kids, growing old, but living, certainly.

It wasn't that she'd assumed they'd get back together. But she had expected him to remain a part of her life—to always be there in case she wanted to see him, like the Sky Tower or the geysers in Rotorua. And the thought of him not being there—of not being able to pick up a phone and hear his voice if she'd chosen to—hurt more than she thought possible.

When he finally ran out of steam, Neve was waiting for him at the chairlift. He hopped off, slid down the slight slope, and came to a stop before her.

"That was fucking amazing." He lifted his goggles onto his hat to reveal shining eyes and flushed cheeks. His hair stuck up from beneath the hat, and his lips still bore her pink lip balm.

She walked up to him and slid her arms around his waist. The bulky jacket meant she couldn't feel him much, but when his arms came around her and squeezed her, it made it worthwhile.

"What's this for?" He kissed the top of her head.

She cleared her throat and released him. "It was good to watch you, that's all. It took me back."

He dropped his arms, reluctantly, she thought. "Yeah, me too. I haven't worked out like that for a long time. Fell on my arse once or twice so I'm going to have a few bruises." He unstrapped his boots and lifted them off the snowboard.

"Need me to rub them better?"

He straightened, and his hazel eyes surveyed her, turning hot and sultry in a matter of seconds. "Oh yeah."

Her heart raced. "Come on, then." Grabbing his hand, she led him up toward the resort.

The snow season had only just started, and although there were several coach loads of visitors, most of them were out on the slopes, watching the bigger runs, or in the restaurant that overlooked the valley. Neve led him across to the kiosk where they handed in their snowboards and helmets, then took him past the restaurant to the block of dressing rooms.

They retrieved their clothing from the lockers, then, after checking to make sure that nobody was watching, she opened the door of one of the rooms and pulled him inside.

He laughed as she locked the door behind him, and he pulled her into his arms. "There isn't a lot of room to maneuver," he whispered.

She kissed him. "There's enough for what I want to do."

Chapter Seventeen

Rhett couldn't have been more surprised. He'd thought he would have to convince Neve to sleep with him again—maybe have another evening of dinner and conversation to thaw the icy barrier she kept around herself. So when she pressed him up against the wall of the changing room and claimed his mouth, for a moment he just stood there, shocked, his senses spinning.

Being out on the slopes had been an utter joy. Although he still played badminton, went to the gym, and ran most days, he'd forgotten the sheer bliss of snowboarding, the way it felt to give himself over to the board and use his weight and balance to guide him over the jumps and jibs. His muscles felt loose, and he'd been hot inside the snow suit in spite of the freezing weather, although his hands and face were cold even though he'd worn gloves and goggles.

Now his senses didn't know what to feel, as Neve's warm mouth covered his own, her tongue sliding against his and turning his inner thermostat up to sizzling. He murmured his approval and cupped her head, and they exchanged a long, slow kiss that had his heart banging against his ribs and his erection springing to life inside his trousers. Was she really hoping to go all the way in this tiny room? He'd barely be able to get his jacket off without banging his elbows on the walls. Not that he was complaining. Whatever she wanted, he was happy to comply.

Catching the tag of the zipper on his jacket, she tugged it down to the bottom, then pushed it off his shoulders. He caught it in his hands and hung it on the peg, then did the same to hers. Beneath their jackets, he wore a thin fleece top over a wicking layer, although under his ski pants he only wore one wicking fleece layer because he'd known he'd get hot once he started on the slopes. Neve had done the same, by the look of it, and he went to remove her fleece top, but she knocked his hands away.

She took off his boots and removed his ski pants, leaving him standing there in just his fleece clothing. Placing one hand on his chest, she pushed him up against the door. Then, before he could object or ask what she had in mind, she kissed his neck, his chest, and slowly down his body as she sank onto her knees.

Rhett's eyebrows rose, and his jaw dropped. Was she really...? Oh yeah. She was. She tugged down his fleece trousers, and he felt a touch of embarrassment as his erection strained toward her through his boxer-briefs like a hungry tiger trying to reach its prey through a cage.

"Sorry," he said, "I'm a bit keyed up."

"Don't apologize." She caressed him through the fabric, and as she did so, she leaned forward and placed a kiss on the scar that was just visible above his underwear.

He rested a hand on her head. He'd seen her eyes glistening when he'd walked up to her outside, and he'd guessed by the way she'd thrown her arms around him that she'd been thinking about his illness. It must have been a shock for her, and it would take her a while to process the implications behind it—God knew it had taken him months.

She slipped her fingers into the elastic of his boxers and lifted them over his erection and down his legs. He heard her inhale, and then her fingers closed around his shaft and she began to stroke.

Rhett leaned his head back on the door and closed his eyes, trying not to groan out loud. He didn't quite succeed when she finally lowered her mouth and enclosed the tip. The sensations were so extreme—the cold breeze that blew in through the rooms each time the front door opened, her hot mouth, her cool fingers on his skin, and the blood that raced around his body, superheating every cell until he burned for her.

She'd always been good at oral, and clearly she hadn't lost her touch. He felt her tongue slide across the head, and then she took him deep inside her mouth, encasing him in hot, wet heat. He looked down, torn between wanting to close his eyes and concentrate on the sensations she was arousing in him, or watching her lips slide down the shaft and her tongue tease the tip.

She glanced up at him, the sexy taunt in her eyes such a turn on, and he slipped a hand into her hair, unable to stop himself holding her tightly as he pushed deeper into her mouth. She let him, murmuring her encouragement, and nudged his thighs, forcing him to widen his stance.

Lifting her head, she whispered. "Do you mind if I touch you here? If you'd rather I didn't..."

"I don't mind."

While she continued to stroke him with her left hand, she moved her right between his legs and gently cupped him.

Rhett leaned his head back again, trying to remember to breathe, and let her explore. He concentrated on enjoying the sensations, liking her gentle touch, her light fingers stroking, and the erotic suction of her mouth on his sensitive skin.

He wasn't far from coming, which was both fantastic and disappointing at the same time, as he wanted it to go on forever. At that moment, however, she lifted her head, and he looked down to watch as she dropped a hand to her own waistband and slipped it beneath the elastic and down between her legs.

Was she going to arouse herself while she went down on him? He would be very happy with that. But after a moment, she brought her hand back up and slid it once more between his legs while she lowered her mouth. She'd coated her fingers with her lubrication, and as she used it to explore even deeper he inhaled sharply.

"Fuck." He clenched his hand in her hair. "I said I didn't need my prostate checked. *Aaahhh.*" He banged the back of his head on the door and screwed up his eyes. The sensation was exquisite, though, not at all what he'd expected. Combined with the feeling of her sucking hard, it was enough to make heat rush through him. His body went rigid as his muscles clenched and pulsed and forced jet after jet of fluid into her eager mouth, and he had to bite his lip hard to stop himself from groaning out loud.

It took a few dizzying moments for the world to stop spinning, and then he tugged her hair. She withdrew her fingers and pushed herself up, kissing back up his body until she reached his mouth.

"Don't even think about it," he warned her.

She kissed him anyway, stifling his protestations, still stroking his softening erection with a careful hand.

He gave in and let her, filled with immense wellbeing at that moment.

"Mmm," he murmured when she eventually drew back. "You little minx."

She chuckled and lifted his boxers up, and he tugged up his fleece pants. Then he pulled her into his arms and gave her a long hug.

"Thank you," she whispered, resting her cheek on his chest.

"Thank you? For what?"

"For letting me touch you."

He'd been right—this was about more than just sex. She'd been upset, and she'd wanted to show him how she felt, because she couldn't put it into words.

"It's okay." He rubbed her back. "You shouldn't be sad. It's one of those things. It's life."

"I know. But it makes me think about how I'd have felt if I'd refused to speak to you, and you'd... died."

"But I didn't die, Neve." He kissed her hair. "You have to stop worrying about things that haven't happened."

She didn't reply, but she shook a little in his arms.

"Come on," he murmured. "It's cold in here. Why don't we get dressed and go have something to eat and drink?"

"Okay."

Oddly subdued, she let him help her get dressed, and then—after making her wash her hands—he returned their ski clothing and led her into the restaurant.

He'd hoped to keep her to himself so they could talk more, but a group from the conference beckoned them over, and it seemed rude to refuse. In the end they had a pleasant time, though. They ordered a toasted chicken panini and fries each and washed it down with a beer, and even though she didn't wolf her food down quite as fast as him, she did finish it, and by the end had a bit more color in her cheeks.

Shortly afterward, it was time to go to the distillery, so they bundled back into the coach and set off.

They'd only been traveling about five minutes when Neve's phone rang.

"Sorry." She took it out of her pocket, looked at the screen, and sighed. "It's Deana."

Rhett watched her, wondering if she'd just turn the phone off, but she didn't, swiping the screen and pressing it to her ear.

"Hi, Deana."

She began to talk with her sister. He tried not to eavesdrop, but it was difficult when she was sitting right next to him. The conversation appeared to consist of Deana trying to talk Neve into going to see her father, and Neve interjecting with sporadic, flat refusals.

Rhett wondered whether part of what Neve was feeling had anything to do with her father. Maybe what she'd said about wondering how she would have felt if she'd refused to speak to Rhett and he'd died had brought up similar issues with her dad. Rhett could understand that. There was no doubt that he'd changed in many ways since his illness. He no longer saw the point in bearing a grudge, and although his old temper hadn't completely disappeared, he was far more likely to forgive and forget than to harbor a resentment he knew would eat away at him.

He listened to her curt, clipped words, feeling for her. What her father had said would not be easy for her to forgive. Part of him wanted to go around and punch the guy's lights out. She was obviously tired of her dad talking down to her and was determined to teach him a lesson, and Rhett could understand that. But sometimes, you couldn't change a person no matter how you tried. Was it best to ignore someone who'd hurt you and run the risk that something might happen to them, and then you'd never be able to put it right? Or should you try to make up with them, even though they'd hurt you badly?

There had been a time when Rhett had thought she would never speak to him again. Indeed, right up until he'd seen her in the restaurant on the first day of the conference, he'd expected her to turn around and walk out. The fact that she'd stayed told him she was tired of bearing all that resentment, and maybe she was ready to move on.

Did moving on mean just talking to him and having this fun fling while they were away? Or would she ever want anything more?

She snapped a goodbye and slid her phone back into her pocket, then stared moodily out of the window.

"What are you going to do?" he asked after a while.

She gave a long sigh. "I don't know. If I see him again, isn't that giving in? Isn't it telling him that it was okay to talk to me the way he did?"

"Has Deana spoken to him?"

"No. He refuses to talk about it. She said Mum's told her that he's really upset and is sorry, but that's not good enough, is it? How do I know whether one of them is not just saying that to smooth things over? I'm almost as cross with her for not standing up for me as I am with him."

Rhett reached out and took her hand in his own. "Maybe you need to talk to him again and explain how you feel."

"I can't help but think it would disintegrate into a slanging match. I can't imagine him just sitting there and taking it, can you?"

"How about writing it down, then? Explaining it on paper. Saying how he hurt your feelings, and that you want to make up with him but that you can't let him speak to you like that."

She considered it, her bottom lip sticking out in an attractive pout, making him want to kiss it. "Maybe. Ultimately, though, I don't think he'll ever say what I want to hear."

"Which is?" He waited for her to say *I love you.*

"Sorry." She looked out of the window, at the snow-covered fields flashing by.

Rhett leaned back, glad she hadn't removed her hand from his. Unfortunately, he had no comfort to give her, because he thought she was probably right. The problem was that Brian Clark didn't believe he'd done wrong. He didn't like how his daughter stood up to him, and he disliked the way she lived her life. Because he was her father, he felt it gave him the power to control her and to tell her what to do.

There was more than a little of Brian in Neve, Rhett thought. Stubborn. Proud. Refusing to give way because she had her beliefs, and she thought that if someone didn't think the same way, then they were wrong and deserved to be cut out of her life. Rhett himself had suffered because of it.

But the ice queen had thawed a little, there was no doubt about it. For the first time since he'd known her, she was questioning herself and beginning to doubt her previously firm convictions. While he didn't want her to lose any of her spirit, he hoped she would be able to make up with her father.

Because if she made up with her father, then maybe there was hope for Rhett, too.

Chapter Eighteen

Neve had a knot in her stomach that wouldn't go away.

It had begun when she'd watched Rhett out on the slopes, and the phone call with Deana had only served to intensify it. It was becoming difficult to get rid of the feeling that she'd screwed up her life. How could that be possible? She hadn't forced Rhett to accept the placement on the Commonwealth team. She hadn't been responsible for their break-up, or for his illness. And she certainly hadn't been responsible for her father's outburst on Christmas Day.

So why did she feel as if everything was her fault?

She wasn't used to the feeling. When something went wrong, she always comforted herself by analyzing what had happened and convincing herself there was nothing she could have done. Rhett had made an unfair decision without consulting her, and she could no more have rolled over and let him believe he was right than flown to the Moon. It was the same with her father—how could she beg his forgiveness for walking out when she couldn't have done anything else after he'd insulted her?

Rhett squeezed her hand. "Try to relax. We're a long way from him now. Don't let him spoil your time away."

She hadn't realized she'd tensed up. "That's true," she conceded. "This trip was supposed to be an escape from everything, some time on my own to reevaluate."

He pulled an *eek* face. "Sorry."

She nudged his shoulder. "I didn't mean you. Although I have to admit, this is not how I saw the conference turning out."

"Me neither." But he gave a happy grin and looked as if he wasn't displeased with the way it had gone. "So," he said, bending closer so his mouth was next to her ear. "Have you had any more thoughts on your remote control? I need to pay you back for the dressing room."

She shivered—from the memory of having him in her mouth, the idea of him having control over her arousal, and the warmth of his breath on her skin. "I haven't decided."

"Can I try to persuade you?"

"No coercing, Rhett. I know we've just been, um, intimate, but that was more out of… I don't know, sadness I guess."

"A pity blow job?" He shrugged. "Better than nothing."

"Rhett!"

"What?"

"You're so…"

"Amusing? Handsome? Witty?"

She gave up. "I'm just saying that what happened last night was a one-off, or supposed to be anyway. It was lovely, and I'm so glad we're friends again, but we shouldn't make things harder on ourselves by letting it happen again."

"Shouldn't we?"

She frowned. "What do you mean?"

"I mean yes, it *was* lovely, and it makes me sad to think we won't be doing it again. I know you don't want anything long term, but it seems a shame that we're not going to make the most out of this time away, now that we've jumped the hurdle and gotten together. Why only do it the once? You said it's nice that we're friends again. Imagine what good friends we'd be if we had sex a few more times."

She had to laugh at his male logic. "You make a good point."

"Think about it." They were pulling up at the distillery, and he reached above their heads for the jackets they'd removed for the journey and handed hers to her. "I'm here if you want me."

His words rang in her head as she tugged on the blue jacket, her blue bobble hat, and a thick, fawn-colored scarf. Rhett wore a padded gray jacket and a patterned woolen scarf that looked as if his mum had bought it for him, which she probably had, Neve mused with a smile. He'd been close to his mum even before his dad died—presumably his father's death and his own illness had brought them even closer together.

They exited the coach and followed everyone else over to the gray buildings that reminded her of the stonework she'd seen in the Peak District in England. There they were divided into groups and given a tour of the distillery, and shown how the malted barley was milled, added to pure alpine water and yeast, mashed, fermented, then distilled in copper pot stills from Scotland before being made into vodka, whisky, and liqueurs. They were shown the sherry casks from

Spain and the bourbon casks from the United States, and then finally led into the bar.

Here they had a wonderful tasting session, and Neve knew the smell of malted cereal would always bring her back to this evening—freezing cold outside with the snow falling thickly on the darkening fields, but everything oh-so-warm inside as the real log fires threw up flames that made the polished mahogany tables and the terracotta floor tiles glow in the lamplight. She would remember the glug of amber liquid being poured into her shining glass with its heavy base, and it would make her think of the way Rhett looked at her, the heat in his eyes making her burn the same way as the whisky when it set fire to her insides.

To her surprise, she enjoyed the company too. People were starting to make friends and form groups, gravitating toward each other whenever they sat, and she found herself sitting with Lisa—whom she was actually starting to like—and some of the other speakers, as well as a few of the attendees. Conversation and laughter flowed along with the drinks, and although she'd started the course thinking she'd find everyone irritating, she discovered that the majority of people had a decent sense of humor, and everyone was willing to share tales of their businesses without being boring.

"Why do they spell it whisky without an 'e'?" Lisa wanted to know. "I thought it was always spelled whiskey."

"Because they use Scottish two-row barley, which makes it Scotch whisky, without an 'e', not Irish whiskey with one," Rhett said.

Neve rolled her eyes. "You're such a know-all."

"Hey. We can't all be geniuses." He put his arm around her shoulder, pulled her to him, and kissed her cheek. He'd never been the type to mark his territory, so she was sure it was a natural, unthinking gesture of affection.

A few of the others smiled, but nobody said anything, and Neve realized they must have assumed she and Rhett were a couple. Why? Had someone seen him coming to her room the night before? Lisa smiled and winked at her before turning to talk to someone else, which made Neve suspect she might be the root of the information.

She thought it would have irritated her that everyone assumed they were together, but oddly, it didn't. It had been a long time since she'd been out with someone with whom she felt comfortable being around like she did with Rhett. They'd slipped easily into the groove of their old relationship, and it surprised her how good it made her feel.

Rhett, too, looked at ease and happy. Relaxed and mellow from a good afternoon's workout, with a glass of whisky in his hand, he was on top form, telling stories, being amusing, winning everyone over—men and women alike—with his wit, his charm, and the sheer force of his personality.

She'd forgotten—how could she have forgotten?—just how good he was with people. How he looked at you and made you feel as if you were the only person in the room. How he had the ability to make anyone—everyone—think he was fascinated with what they had to say. And it wasn't all an act either; he genuinely seemed interested in people, and he knew just how to draw everyone into the conversation, how to make even the quietest at the table feel included.

He's not perfect, she scolded herself. She mustn't start putting him on a pedestal, or they'd both come crashing down in an awkward tangle of limbs. Although energetic ninety percent of the time, the other ten percent he was lazy, and he hated doing household chores. He refused to pick up an iron and only bought clothes guaranteed to be able to wash and wear. He hated losing—at anything—and everyone knew better than to start a game of Trivial Pursuit with him.

At least, that was how he used to be. Was he the same now? Neve couldn't be sure any more. It was like being shown into a house she'd lived in for years in her youth and that she was sure she knew like the back of her hand, only to find the furniture had all changed, the walls had been re-painted, and none of the doors were where they used to be.

"You're quiet," he murmured to her when the manager of the distillery stopped by their table to answer any questions the group had. "Are you still thinking about your father?"

"No," she said truthfully. "About you."

"Oh?" He curled a strand of her hair around his finger. "Tell me."

She leaned her head on a hand, her muscles aching a little from the exercise, but otherwise feeling relaxed and content. "I'm wondering how much you've changed."

"Not at all. Sausages are still my favorite food."

"Like a dog," she said, and smiled. "You have changed, though. You're different… more thoughtful… more grown up. You were such a hothead when we were young. You had such a temper."

His lips twisted wryly. "Yeah. Everything seemed so important and intense, and it all mattered so much."

"And nothing matters now?"

He tipped his head from side to side. "I've learned not to sweat the small stuff, that's all. I fight the battles worth fighting, and if I can't do anything about it, I let it pass."

"I don't know how to do that," she whispered. "I wish I did."

"I know." He picked up another strand of her hair and ran his fingers down it. "Like ribbon," he mused, twisting it around.

"You're so open," she said. "It's like you're walking around on a battlefield wearing only a pair of underpants, and I'm in full plate armor."

He laughed. "Sounds like a bad dream."

"I mean it. I feel as if I have to protect myself all the time. I worry that if I don't, someone's going to reach right inside my chest and rip out my heart."

"That happens when you've been hurt," he said easily. "It's understandable."

"But why aren't you like that?"

"I was. For a long time. But illness changes you, Neve. All that resentment, hatred, and anger—it just feeds on itself. It's like the cancer. It eats away at all the good stuff until there's only the bad left."

He swirled what was left of his whisky around the glass. "A few months into the treatment, I was lying on the hospital bed, angry at myself for getting sick, at my father for passing on the gene, at you, my coach, at the world for my terrible luck. I was tired and unhappy, because I couldn't tell at the time how it was all going to work out. I didn't know how having testicular cancer and having an operation would make others—women, mainly—react to me. I felt as if the world was against me."

His hazel eyes had caught the glow of the fire, and they'd warmed to the same amber as the whisky in his glass. "I was dozing, and I don't know what happened, but I had a… revelation, I suppose you could call it. Not religious or anything like that. But in that strange state between being asleep and being awake, I suddenly understood. Nobody was against me. I wasn't being *done to*."

He hesitated, frowning. Normally, Neve would have teased him at that point for waffling and not knowing what he was talking about, but this time she held back, conscious that he was opening up to her, confessing something he might not have told anyone else.

"What I mean is," he continued, "I understood at that moment that the anger I'd felt, the resentment, every time I got irritated or cross or frustrated, it had built up inside me and was making me as sick as the cancer. Sick to my soul. Does that make sense?"

Neve thought about it for a moment, conscious of everything around them fading into the background. Outside, the snow was blanketing the path and making the sheep blend in with the fields, but her cheeks were warm from the whisky and the fire. She felt all mixed up, confused by this new, thoughtful Rhett, who would have laughed at such nonsense in the past.

"Maybe it doesn't," he said, apparently taking her lack of response as a negative. "I don't really know what I'm trying to say. I did my best to let go of the things that frustrated me. And I try not to harbor resentment or get angry. It doesn't always work—if my computer won't start, I'm still tempted to throw it across the room. But I don't anymore. And I'm a better person for it, I think."

"I envy you," Neve said, then hastily added, "I don't mean with the cancer—that was a terrible thing to say. I'm sorry."

He smiled. "It's all right."

"I meant the way you've reinvented yourself. I'd like to do that, but I don't know if it's possible without the kind of event you've experienced, something that makes you look at life in a completely different way."

"I think it helps, but I don't see why everyone can't do it. You've got to want to change. It's about a shift in perception. Seeing the glass as half full not half empty. Not focusing on what's going wrong, but on what's going right. Celebrating what you have, and not always reaching for what you don't. Making the most of every opportunity that's available to you, because you don't know when it will come around again."

Neve didn't reply, concentrating on finishing off her drink. She couldn't see how it was possible to change the way you were like that, not without some big, life-changing experience. It felt as if she'd been frustrated and irritable forever—but that was just who she was. If a person was a pessimist, or arrogant, or a snob, was it possible for them to become an optimist? Could you train yourself not to be arrogant, or not to look down your nose at things? Rhett had definitely changed, but she couldn't help but think it was either the shock of his illness or a physical effect of the treatment that had changed him on more than an emotional level. Maybe the radiotherapy had screwed with his hormones, or changed the way his neurons interacted.

Whatever the reason, she couldn't see how she could just start being open and trusting of people. It wasn't in her nature. She was doomed to stay the way she was for the rest of her life, and she just had to get used to it.

Chapter Nineteen

People were beginning to stir, and it was obviously time to go back to the hotel, so they returned their glasses to the bar, donned their jackets, and made their way outside. Night had settled on the landscape, and from the hushed silence Neve could tell that snow had carpeted the hillsides for miles.

"Will the coach be all right on the journey back?" she asked as they boarded.

"They'll have salted the roads." Rhett lowered himself into the seat beside her. "Don't worry—if we were a month later we might have had trouble, but we'll be fine."

She drew up her legs and wrapped her arms around them, resting her head against the window. His words circled in her head as if they were on a merry-go-round. *Making the most of every opportunity that's available to you, because you don't know when it will come around again.* Her lips twisted. He'd probably said that to get in her knickers. But even if he had, he'd unknowingly struck a chord. She didn't know that she could change the way she was at heart, but she could be brave and take a step out of her comfort zone. She'd already slept with him once. What did it matter to anyone but the two of them if they slept together again? He was hot, and he was good at it, and while they were away, it was as if time and the past didn't matter. When they returned to Wellington, they'd have to figure out a way to be around each other again, but maybe he was right and their new closeness would make them better friends.

"Penny for them," he said, bumping her shoulder.

She turned her gaze from the snowy scene to look at him. "Take out your phone."

He stared at her for a long moment, and then slowly a beautiful smile spread across his face, so warm and sexy it made her ache. He slid the phone out of the pocket of his jeans and swiped the screen.

"Find this app." She told him what to search for, and he located it and began downloading it.

"What changed your mind?" he said softly while he waited.

"You did. You're right. These opportunities don't come around very often. We've been too long not friends, and it was as if we've been given these few days to make up for that. I don't see why we can't put everything aside and just concentrate on right here, right now."

Was it her imagination, or did a hard glint appear in his eye? If it did, he hid it by glancing down at his phone and opening the app. He thumbed through the instructions, then switched off the phone and slid it back in his pocket. His smile reappeared as he looked back at her. "So what's the plan?"

She shrugged, following his lead and speaking softly so those sitting around them wouldn't be able to hear. "I'll go to my room and... um... apply it. Then you get to activate it."

He looked amused. "So you're going to go to dinner and listen to a marketing talk in front of hundreds of people while you're wearing a vibrator that I control?"

"Well, now you put it like that, maybe it's not such a good idea." Her heart picked up pace at the thought. Jeez. Was she really thinking of handing over control of her arousal to him?

"I think it's a fucking marvelous idea. I can't wait."

Her lips curved up. "Don't get too carried away. It's not like I'm going to be able to relax enough to come in the middle of the restaurant."

"We'll see."

Her eyes widened. "Rhett! For God's sake."

"I'll have you begging me to let you come before midnight," he murmured.

She gave a short laugh. "Yeah, right. That'll be the day."

He moved closer to her. "Wanna bet?"

She looked into his eyes. He was excited about the idea, turned on by the thought of being in charge. Doubt flickered inside her. Why did everyone always want to control her? And why the hell did the thought of it turn her on so much?

"I'm not sure about this." Her mouth had gone dry.

"Relax." He lifted a finger and ran it across her brow to remove a strand of hair, a strangely tender gesture. "Stop worrying so much. It's not about me controlling you."

"How did you know that's what I was thinking?"

"It's written all over your face." He touched a finger to her nose. "It's just a bit of fun, Neve. You can walk out at any time. Or, I'll tell you what—why don't we have a safe word? If you truly want me to stop, just say it and I promise I will. Hand on my heart." He illustrated his words.

She moistened her lips. "Okay. What's the word?"

"You decide."

"Um... how about... whisky?"

"Ah, probably not a good idea since we're supposed to be evaluating the marketing plan of a distillery."

"Oh, right. Okay, what about... mountain."

He smiled. "Mountain it is."

She felt better at his promise that he'd stop if she wanted him to. That gave her a little control back, at least.

They crossed the bridge over the Shotover River and followed the finger of water known as the Frankton Arm toward Queenstown. The water looked like icy black glass, the slopes of the forested hills just dark shadows against the even darker sky.

"Spooky," she said with a shiver.

Rhett chuckled. "Do you think so? I've always thought the place cozy. Like the hills are protecting it."

She mused on that as they entered the town, the roads becoming lined with houses and shops that lent a glow to the night. Some of them had colored lights to celebrate the midwinter festival. The town was still bustling, people heading home after finishing work and late-night shopping, and as they left the coffee shops and clothing stores behind and neared Marine Parade, Neve could see what he meant. Nobody who lived here thought the place spooky. Was a dark shape in the shadows threatening you or protecting you from the even darker night? It was all to do with how you looked at things, and it gave her a lot to think about.

It wasn't long before they pulled up out the front of the hotel. They exited the bus, exclaiming as they found themselves ankle-deep in snow, the light dusting having morphed into thicker, heavier flakes that were settling all over the town.

"Thirty minutes until dinner," Lisa called as everyone scurried into the warmth of the hotel foyer.

Neve shook the snow off her hat, watching Rhett brush it off his hair.

"See you at dinner," she whispered.

He grinned. "Text me when you've fitted it, eh?"

"Okay." Giving him one last, heated look, she left and went up to her room.

Once inside, she took fifteen minutes to freshen up and change into a pair of soft black pants and a scarlet shirt. As she stood in front of the mirror to apply her makeup, she noted that her cheeks were already flushed, although whether it was from the sun she'd caught on the slopes or the excitement of anticipating the evening to come, she couldn't tell. She smudged some smoky gray shadow on her lids, brushed some black mascara on her lashes, and added sparkly red gloss to her lips. She left her hair down, ruffled and loose, and stepped back to admire the look.

It was nice to see the dark shadows gone from her eyes and color in her cheeks. She had a vibrancy about her that had been missing for too long, she thought. It couldn't all be down to Rhett, though. She was discovering lots of interesting and useful information for her business, and just generally having a good time. The great sex was an added bonus.

Finally, she found the vibrator at the bottom of her case and took it out of the packet. It was a strange elongated U shape, designed to stimulate both the clitoris and the G-spot. She went into the bathroom and pulled down her trousers and panties. Then, a little nervously, she added a touch of lube to the device and slid the G-spot part of the vibrator inside. The top part fit over her clit as she did so, the whole device kind of 'clipping on', and with some surprise she found it quite snug.

After pulling up her panties and trousers, she practiced walking around the bedroom and then sat gingerly, pleased to find that it felt odd but not uncomfortable. Could she really wear it all evening, though? Only time would tell.

Taking out her phone, she texted Rhett, *Done!* Pressing send, she waited for his reply.

Almost immediately, he texted back. *Cool! Hey did you know this thing has ten modes? Going to try one now. Get ready.*

She giggled and nibbled her bottom lip as she waited. Then, all of a sudden, it buzzed. It made her jump, and she laughed out loud, then closed her eyes as it pulsed against her clit half a dozen times, gradually growing in intensity until she exhaled with a long groan. It stopped then, and her phone announced another text.

I can turn it up too :-) What do you think?

Fuck me, she exclaimed on the screen, blowing out a breath.

Is that an order?

She laughed. *Maybe. See you in a minute.*

He just texted *xx*.

She stood, aware of her heart racing. Holy crap. Suddenly she wasn't so sure of her insistence that he couldn't make her come in public. He wouldn't though, would he? He'd stop before she got that far. She had to remember her safe word and use it if it became unbearable.

Mountain, she thought as she picked up her bag and made her way out of the room. *Mountain, mountain, mountain.* She had to make sure she didn't forget it!

She went to the ground floor and walked across the foyer, spotting Rhett waiting for her in the doorway.

"Evening," he said.

"Hello." Her cheeks grew warm. Good grief. Was she blushing again?

He observed her with much amusement. "Blushing, Clark?" He leaned closer to murmur in her ear, his breath warm on her skin. "Or is that the flush of sexual pleasure I can see?"

"Stop it." She was almost breathless with lust and nervousness. Even when she was walking, the vibrator aroused all her sensitive bits, and it was only made worse having him there and knowing that at any moment he could turn it on. This was going to be a nightmare.

To her surprise, though, they went into the restaurant, joined a table, and were served their starter and main course, and Rhett didn't touch the vibrator once. She sent him a couple of puzzled glances across the table, but each time he just lifted his eyebrows as if to say *What?* Had he forgotten, she wondered? Surely not. No, he was biding his time, sending her into a sexual haze at the sheer anticipation of when he was going to start. The more that time wore on without him using it, the more turned on she got. How was that possible? Every time she looked at him and saw him observing her with lust-filled eyes, she could feel her body preparing itself for him, moistening, swelling, wanting his touch. Holy moly. She was going to come and he wouldn't even have to touch the fucking vibrator.

The waiters collected their empty dinner plates, topped up their wine glasses, then delivered the desserts as John Lyttleton took the podium and began his talk on marketing in New Zealand, drawing on examples from the ski resort and the distillery to illustrate. The mood of the room was jovial, with everyone tired from their day in the fresh air but buoyed up by the excellent food and wine and the great company.

Neve sipped her wine, listening to Lyttleton as she picked up her spoon and admired the fresh fruit Pavlova in her dish. Created in honor of the Russian ballerina Anna Pavlova, the meringue-based dessert was claimed by the Australians to have originated over the Ditch, as they called the Tasman Sea, but all New Zealanders knew it was a Kiwi dessert. To illustrate that, the chef had topped the meringue with slices of kiwi fruit, as well as seasonal blackberries for color.

She dipped her spoon in the meringue and raised it to her mouth. At that moment, Rhett chose to activate the remote control, and a moderate buzz emitted from the vibrator, luckily silent, but strong enough to make her drop her spoon into her dish with a clatter.

Everyone on the table looked around, and she burst out laughing, covering her mouth with a hand so she didn't interrupt Lyttleton's talk. "Sorry," she whispered to Carol, sitting on her right. "I thought I saw a spider."

"Yuck." Carol shuddered. "Nasty. No wonder you jumped."

Neve picked up her spoon again, only then raising her gaze to meet Rhett's. He was grinning, and he chuckled as she looked up and glared at him.

Now she knew his game, she prepared herself for the next buzz. The sneaky bastard wasn't playing fair, though. He waited another five minutes, until she'd finished her dessert and was on the verge of relaxing, before turning it on again just briefly. She'd just taken a mouthful of wine, and she thanked her lucky stars that she didn't spurt it all over the table.

Wiping delicately under her bottom lip, she placed the glass down and leaned back in her chair as inconspicuously as possible. This time, she didn't have to wait so long. Rhett set the vibrator to some kind of wave mode that grew stronger and then fainter in turn, and this time he left it on for longer, fixing his gaze on her, his own chest rising and falling fast enough to tell her that it was turning him on too.

She closed her eyes, hoping it looked as if she was concentrating on the speaker, and sucked her bottom lip, ripples of pleasure radiating through her. She had to be careful to remember where she was and not moan out loud, but it was difficult. The device hit completely the right spots, and the two-pronged attack meant there was no escape.

The vibrating stopped, and she exhaled in a silent sigh and opened her eyes. Rhett was watching her, and his smile had faded. Instead, raw desire filled his eyes, taking her breath away.

He obviously had his phone in his lap, because she saw him glance down at it briefly, and then the pulses started again, this time a series of short, sharp buzzes, immediately followed by an undulating wave of high and low pressure.

She was starting to lose the plot. It was becoming more and more difficult not to exclaim out loud each time it started vibrating, and she was getting to the point where she almost didn't care whether anyone was watching—she wasn't going to be able to stop the orgasm from rolling over her, she was sure.

He was making the pulses closer together but giving shorter bursts, drawing out the pleasure, until she thought she might scream each time he stopped it. She was going to have to stop him. She was in public, for Christ's sake—she couldn't just come in the middle of a lecture. She wouldn't be able to stop herself from crying out, and how embarrassing would that be?

The safe word... what the fuck was it? Her brain wasn't functioning. The pulses seemed to be intensifying, and she realized that was probably due to her arousal, the device tightening on her swollen flesh.

She opened her eyes and looked pleadingly into Rhett's.

He studied her for a long moment, then glanced down and turned the vibrator off. Then, to her surprise, he stood and walked around the table to her chair. He bent down and murmured something to Carol, who nodded and gave her a concerned glance, and then he took Neve's hand and led her out of the restaurant.

Chapter Twenty

Rhett led Neve across the foyer to the elevators and pressed the button.

"What did you say to Carol?"

He turned to look at her, his heart pounding. "I said you were feeling unwell." It had been an easy lie because she didn't look herself—her cheeks were flushed, her eyelids heavy, her blue eyes feverish. Jesus, he wanted to throw her on the floor and fuck her right there in the foyer. He didn't, though. He waited impatiently for the carriage to arrive then pulled her inside and pressed the button to close the doors. After choosing her floor, he thrust her up against the mirrored wall of the carriage, chose one of the buttons on his phone, and as she gasped, he took advantage of her open mouth and kissed her.

He didn't hold back, plunging his tongue into her mouth, and he pushed his hips to hers, feeling the buzzing of her vibrator against the erection that was already raring to go and had been ever since she'd first closed her eyes in ecstasy at the table.

Neve moaned deep in her throat, and he moved back and touched his phone. She sagged against the wall, exhausted, and he felt a brief sweep of pity for her. Not enough to give her the climax she was craving though.

"How long are you going to keep this going?" she said, panting.

"As long as it takes you to beg me." He felt a little mad, his blood superheated until his body burned and his erection throbbed.

"I won't." She lifted her chin and glared at him.

"Fine." He turned the vibrator on again for a few seconds, then switched it off.

"Shiiiiiit." Her head fell back on the wall and she dropped a hand between her thighs to press against the vibrator.

"Stop it." He yanked her hands away and pinned them above her head.

"Rhett..." She ran her tongue along her bottom lip and moaned, and he kissed her again, claiming rather than requesting, taking what he wanted. Her curvy body shivered beneath him, and not for the first time he wondered what underwear she was wearing tonight. Virginal white? Saucy black? Lacy or silky? Suddenly, he was desperate to see.

The elevator dinged and the doors opened. He caught her hand and half led, half dragged her along to her door, took her keycard from her hand, and swiped it.

She went in before him but just stood in the center of the room, dropping her handbag to the floor as if she'd forgotten she was holding it.

Rhett let the door close behind him and walked toward her. She looked stunning, lit by the streetlight that slanted through the window, her lips kissed free of gloss, her hair mussed, her eyes dazed.

He caught a handful of his sweater at the back of his neck, tugged it over his head, and tossed it onto the nearby chair. Then he took hers at the base and lifted that up and off too.

"Rhett..." she whispered, but she didn't seem able to add anything else.

He took off his shirt, then ran a hand around her waist—her trousers appeared to be soft and elasticated, so he tugged them down over her hips and let them fall to the floor. As she stepped out of them, he blew out a long breath at the sight of her scarlet lacy panties.

"That's it." Something flipped inside him. He took both sides of her shirt in his hands and yanked them apart. Buttons flew in all directions, but it meant he had an unobstructed view of her matching scarlet lace bra.

"Rhett!" She squealed and pushed him away, but he wasn't having any of that. He tugged down her panties, then moved toward her, forcing her back against the chest of drawers. Reaching behind her, he swept off the leaflets and knickknacks resting on the top, then lifted her onto the top.

"What the hell are you doing?"

He ignored her and pushed her knees apart, struggling to retain his own composure at the sight of the vibrator pressed to her swollen folds. Without further ado, he retrieved his phone and pressed the button on the app.

She shuddered and arched her back, letting out a long moan. He flicked the vibrator off and leaned either side of her.

"You're so fucking sexy." He kissed her, and she went limp, opening her mouth to his searching tongue. She tried to close her legs, but he stood between them, stopping her, and she mumbled a complaint.

He groaned. "I'm so hot for you." He let his lips play across hers, enjoying the anticipation, the fact that every time he touched her, even with just a brush of his lips, she sighed with longing, and his body throbbed. "And I'm going to have you, in a minute. I can fuck you with the vibrator in, right?"

"Oh… yes… please…" She fumbled at his waist, and he let her undo his belt and unzip his trousers. He had a condom ready, and when she freed his erection, he swiftly rolled the condom on.

She moved to the edge, pulling him toward her, but he shook his head and, with his free hand, pressed the phone and turned the vibrator on again.

"Argh… Rhett!" She tipped back her head and groaned.

He switched it off. She sagged and moved a hand between her legs to try to stimulate herself.

"No." He took both her hands and held them behind her back with one of his, then turned the vibrator on again, setting it to buzz in long waves from gentle to intense pulses. It was going to feel fantastic when he slid inside her, but he wanted to wait.

"Oh… Jesus…" She tensed each time it vibrated and went limp each time it stopped. "Oh God, are you trying to kill me with pleasure?" She tried to yank her hands free, but he was stronger than her, and she soon gave up.

He cupped her breast with his free hand and stroked her nipple through the lace. She opened dazed eyes and looked up at him longingly.

"Beg me," he suggested, bending to brush his lips along her jaw as he tugged on her nipple

"No. Ohhh…"

He placed soft kisses up to her ear, feeling the vibrations stopping, starting, stopping again. He tugged the other nipple, gently, just hard enough to make her groan.

She rested her forehead on his shoulder. "Rhett…"

Her hair fell forward, sleek and shiny, curling around her flushed cheek, and Rhett felt a surge of affection and love for her. He was crazy about this girl—he always would be, and he wanted nothing more than to give her pleasure.

He kissed the top of her head and whispered, "Beg me."

She swallowed, breathing hard, and lifted her face to his. "Please."

It was good enough, because he wasn't far from climaxing either, even though he hadn't touched himself once.

He lifted her chin and kissed her softly, tenderly, then reached for his phone and switched it to a steady vibrate.

He was desperate to take her, but first he wanted to watch the pleasure steal over her. He pushed her knees wide, still holding her hands behind her back, and when she wriggled and tried to writhe against him, he let his lips brush hers and murmured, "Wait. Just let it happen."

She stilled, and he kissed her once more then lifted his head.

It was like watching the sun rise over the horizon, slow and beautiful. He observed the pleasure gathering, watched her hold her breath, felt her stiffen, tighten, and saw the moment it took her over the edge.

She gasped, and at that moment he pressed the tip of his erection between her legs and into her swollen folds. He'd wondered briefly whether he should have used some lubrication, but he needn't have worried. She was extremely wet, and he slid straight in, immediately feeling the buzz of the vibrator against his sensitive skin.

Neve cried out and clamped around him, and he gave in to his urge to thrust and went for it. She wrapped her legs around his waist, and he released her hands and steadied himself on the surface as he thrust hard. She squealed and then gasped out a series of long, sexy moans, but he didn't stop, losing himself in the sensation of plunging into her. The chest of drawers banged against the wall, the handles on the drawers rattled, but neither of them cared, and he hoped to hell there was nobody in the other room as he thrust harder and harder, driven to distraction by the deep buzz of the vibrator and her muscles that still clenched around him.

The climax started in his toes and swept up to the roots of his hair before centering in his groin where it exploded with white-hot heat. He gave a long, heartfelt groan as he came, and was only half aware of Neve's hand clutching his hair, her mouth capturing his exclamations as the intense pulses bore him away.

"Holy fuck." He trembled from the force of the orgasm, then gave a startled "Yow!" as the vibrator continued buzzing on his extremely sensitive skin. He turned it off and withdrew from her carefully, and she removed the vibrator with a groan.

"Come here." He lifted her up, walked to the bed, and fell back onto it, not caring that she sprawled across him.

"Oh my God." She lay there, limp as a softened candle, boneless and exhausted. "I'm never going to be able to move again, ever."

"We'll just have to stay here, then." Spending eternity naked with the girl of his dreams? He could live with that.

"Mmm." She raised a hand to her bra and then dropped it again. "Can you unclip it?"

He moved a lazy hand up to the back strap and flicked it with his fingers. It popped open.

She removed it, casting him a wry glance. "I swear you could open it just by looking at it."

"I'm working on it."

She shifted to his side and curled up to him, warm and still trembling a little.

"Are you okay?" He kissed her hair.

"Yeah. It was intense, that's all."

"I didn't hurt you?"

"Of course not."

Her words implied she didn't think he would ever hurt her. He gave a silent sigh, wishing that were true. She might be stubborn and unforgiving, but she'd only reacted the way she had to what had happened all those years ago because he'd hurt her. He'd tried to tell himself there was no point in having regrets, but that was the one thing in his life he wished he'd done differently.

He wanted to lie like that all night, but the cool room had brought goosebumps out on his skin, and he wanted to get comfortable. "Shall we get under the duvet?" he asked her.

She didn't say anything for a moment, and then she rose up onto an elbow to look at him. She looked so beautiful, silhouetted by the lamplight outside. Her dark hair gleamed, and he reached out to wrap a strand of it around his finger.

"Actually, I think you should go," she said.

Startled, he let the strand of hair drop. "What?"

"It was lovely, Rhett, but I think it would be best if we kept this physical, you know? If we sleep together, it will only make it harder when we get back to Wellington."

Her eyes glinted, flat pieces of hard ice. He was dumbfounded. Literally minutes ago they'd had sex and shared what he thought was an amazing experience. When he'd watched her come, he'd been filled with love for her, and he'd known at that moment that he wanted to be with her forever.

And now she was telling him to walk away?

He stared at her, and she looked out of the window. She didn't want to meet his gaze. She knew what she was doing. She was trying to protect herself. The sex they'd just shared had shaken her to the core—it must have. She knew she was falling for him all over again, and it scared her. She thought that if she sent him away, she'd be able to keep her distance.

He thought about arguing with her, stating that she was being foolish, that she was a coward, and that she needed to man up and work out what she really wanted out of life. But he was tired, and he didn't have the energy for an argument.

"All right." He got up, zipped up his trousers, and pulled on his shirt. Without buttoning it up, he tugged the sweater on over the top.

Neve got to her feet, wrapping the duvet around her, and stood there mutely. She looked a mixture of defensive and lost, and in spite of his irritation that she was sending him away, his heart still went out to her. Maybe she was right—maybe it was impossible to change unless you experienced the kind of life-changing event that he had. She was stuck in the past, and she couldn't seem to lever herself out of the trench, no matter how hard she tried.

He still had one day, though. Once they returned to Wellington, he was certain she'd be lost to him, but although tomorrow would be busy with workshops, there would be time to talk and be together, and then they had the party at the end of the day. He still had time to convince her that she should be with him.

He walked toward her, slid a hand to the back of her head, and held her there while he kissed her. Tenderly this time, a brush of his lips to hers, meant to console, not to arouse.

"Don't fret," he whispered. "I'll see you tomorrow."

She just nodded.

He let his hand fall, walked out of the room, and let the door close behind him.

Chapter Twenty-One

Eight a.m. the next day found Neve standing by the window, looking down at the snow-covered streets of Queenstown. The heavy gray sky looked as if it had another couple of inches of snow just waiting to fall, and people walked with collars turned up and hats pulled over their ears, illustrating the freezing temperature.

She wrapped her arms around herself and leaned her head on the window. She'd slept badly, tormented by images of the evening, her body hankering both physically and emotionally for the man who'd given her such pleasure.

Even now, when she closed her eyes, she could still see him, his hazel eyes burning into hers as he breathed heavily, keeping a tight control on his own desire so he could tease her right to the edge.

She'd forgotten how good he was in bed. All the sex she'd had since they'd broken up seemed like a pale imitation of what she'd experienced with Rhett that evening. It had been fun, and erotic, but it had also been more than that. Something within him recognized and answered the deep desire she had to be… not controlled—she didn't like that word. Influenced, maybe. Or, okay, she could admit it to herself if not to him—dominated.

She didn't understand it. She hated it out of the bedroom, and would give a guy a right hook rather than have him tell her what to do. But with sex, she liked the fight, the struggle, and ultimately, being conquered. Few of the other guys she'd been with had understood—either they'd backed off when she'd challenged them, or they'd gone the other way and treated her badly, which wasn't the point at all.

How did he know the way to reach in and tug at her heartstrings? He only had to look at her with that gleam in his eye that told her he was going to have his own way whether she liked it or not, and she just melted.

Sadness washed over her. What a shame it had all ended so badly. His betrayal had been a hundred times worse because she'd been so in love with him.

And here she was, having sex with him, an inch away from falling for him all over again. If he'd stayed the night, he would have thought she was changing her mind, and she couldn't have that. She still hadn't recovered from the first time he'd broken her heart—she couldn't risk it happening again.

That wasn't the only reason, though. He'd betrayed her, and no amount of time was going to make that go away. Even though he said he'd changed, her heart wouldn't forgive him for what he'd done. It would always be between them, and how long would it be before it resurfaced, like old tree roots poking through new gravel?

She had to take this for what it was—a hot and sexy fling, which had the added bonus in that it had reestablished their friendship, and it meant they would at least be on talking terms when they returned. Their friends would be over the moon that the bad atmosphere that hung over them all whenever the two of them were present had finally lifted.

Her stomach rumbled, and she pushed off the window and headed for the door. She needed a hot coffee and a hearty breakfast, and soon she'd be right as rain. Right as snow. She smiled as she headed out to the elevators. Everything was going to be fine. Rhett knew as well as she did that there was no hope of anything long term developing between them. She'd said, *Just this once, Rhett. Just physical. That's all this is, right?* And he'd replied, *Of course.* He understood the rules. She had to enjoy this hot fling for what it was, and stop obsessing about the future.

Once again, Rhett was already at the breakfast table when she entered the restaurant, and she joined him, Lisa, and the others, ready to exchange the fun banter they'd had the night before. To her surprise, though, although she met a few smiles when she sat, everyone was quiet, and the mood was definitely off.

"What's up?" she asked as she poured herself a glass of orange juice. "Who died?" As soon as she said it, she saw Rhett wince and knew. "Fuck. Scott?"

"Yes," Lisa said. "I'm sorry to have to tell you that he passed away this morning, around six a.m."

"Shit." Neve sat back in her chair, more upset than she thought she'd be at the death of a man she hardly knew. "I'm so sorry about that comment—I didn't think."

"It's okay. None of us suspected it. I mean, obviously we knew he'd had a heart attack, but he was relatively young."

"What happened?" she asked, feeling queasy.

Lisa shrugged. "We're not sure. Complications in surgery was all they'd tell us."

Neve looked across at Rhett. He gave her a You-Never-Know shrug.

Those at the table continued talking around her in low voices as they ate their breakfasts, but Neve had lost her appetite for both food and conversation. She asked for coffee and nibbled on a piece of toast, but couldn't summon the energy for anything more.

She saw Rhett look over at her a few times, but she kept her gaze fixed on her plate, and as soon as seemed polite, she left the table.

He caught up with her in the foyer. "Neve."

She slowed and stopped. "Hi."

"Hey." He put his hands on her upper arms and bent to look into her eyes. "Are you okay? You look… pale."

"You were going to say terrible then, weren't you?"

"Actually fucking awful were the words I'd chosen, but it seemed a bit rude."

She gave a small laugh. "I'm all right."

"You don't look all right." Without asking, he moved closer and wrapped his arms around her.

Neve rested her cheek on his chest, inhaled the scent of warm, clean male, and pretended to herself for a moment that everything was going to be all right.

"I'm sorry about Scott." He stroked her back. "Poor guy."

"He was so young, that's all."

"I know. I'm guessing he didn't take good care of himself. He looked the sort who had high cholesterol and high blood pressure, and he was drinking a lot that evening."

"You take good care of yourself and you still got sick," she whispered.

"Well, yeah. That's different though. Cancer's not a lifestyle illness, as far as we know."

"I guess." She closed her eyes for a moment, wanting to stay like that forever. He made her feel safe. He cared for her, she knew that. She'd missed him so much when he'd gone away. Although the intensity of it had faded over time, the hole in her heart had never closed over.

"It's all right," he murmured, stroking her hair.

She swallowed hard. This was no good. She couldn't let him comfort her like this—it wasn't fair.

Moving back, she gave him a bright smile. "So what's planned for today, then?"

He gave her an appraising look that told her he wasn't fooled by her fake joviality, but just said, "More workshops today. We'll be putting like businesses together so hopefully you can exchange ideas."

"Sounds great. I'll nip up and get my laptop and catch you later, okay?"

He nodded, and she walked away to the elevator and pressed the button to call the carriage. While she waited, she felt his eyes burning into her back and, unbidden, an image arose in her mind of him watching her as she'd come the night before. She glanced over her shoulder and met his gaze. He had his hands in his pockets, and he wore a sleeveless black sweater over a white shirt. Jeez, he looked sexy. It took all the self-control she possessed not to ask him to come up to her room with her.

His lips curved up as if he was thinking the same thing. Luckily, the doors dinged open before she had a chance to contemplate it seriously. She wrinkled her nose at him and went into the carriage, relieved when the doors closed.

One more day. She didn't know whether to cheer or cry.

*

Although Lisa announced the sad news about Scott to the conference that morning, as tended to happen with the human race, everyone talked about it for ten minutes and then got on with their day.

Neve listened to everyone laughing and joking as they moved around the room to get into their groups, wondering why she felt so upset. What was she expecting? That they would call off the course out of respect? That everyone would weep and wail for hours? He wasn't even one of the organizers—he'd just been a guy whose life had briefly touched those at the hotel, and although what had happened was shocking and sad, and no doubt he would cross most people's minds during the day, that would be as deep as their emotions went.

Normally, she would have been the sort of person to harden herself against feeling anything. She would have told herself not to be stupid because she didn't know him, and she couldn't possibly feel upset. But today, she couldn't fight off an overwhelming sadness.

There must be a reason for it, she thought as she joined the table for those with clothing-related businesses. She'd been the first one at Scott's side when he'd felt unwell, but if she were honest with herself, she hadn't liked him that much. It must be more because it had come so out of the blue, and to someone who was relatively young. That, combined with the fact that she was still shaken up from Rhett's revelation, had served to make her feel unsettled. It was like she'd been walking along the top floor of a tall building and then suddenly looked down and found the floors were made of glass. That was all. There was nothing unusual or worrying about it.

She continued to console herself with those thoughts throughout the morning and, in the end, it worked. Every now and again someone would mention Scott, but generally talk was about business, and Neve soon lost herself in the work.

The organizers and speakers rotated around the groups, so for a while Rhett came to sit with them, and she had the opportunity to observe him as he gave suggestions for advertising on social media and other tips. She loved the way people warmed to him. He had a natural ability to make others feel at ease, and he soon had everyone laughing and offering examples of marketing methods they'd employed.

When it was her turn, he watched her with a smile on his lips as she talked to the others, and she was unable to stop the shiver that ran up her spine at the sensation of his eyes on her. She knew he was thinking about having sex with her again. They had one more night here together. She shouldn't. And yet, why not? Why waste the opportunity to have a bit of fun and some hot sex? She knew he'd say yes if she asked him. He was right—why not make the most of an opportunity like this?

When she finished describing some of the advertising she'd done for the Four Seasons, she sat back and glanced across at him. He met her gaze and winked. She let her lips curve up and winked back. He raised his eyebrows—a query, a sexy, hopeful gesture. She slid her gaze down him slowly, imagining stripping off his black sweater, pulling apart his white shirt. He'd ruined hers by popping all the buttons—she was going to have to pay him back for that. Maybe she should tie him to the bed and punish him.

As soon as the thought entered her head, though, she knew it wouldn't work. Rhett wasn't keen on being restrained. If it was the other way around, though… She remembered vividly one time when they'd come home from a party late one night—someone's twenty-first, if she remembered correctly. She'd been cheeky to him that evening, teased him about something in front of their friends, and he'd given her a look that meant *You'll pay for that later*. And she had. He'd tied her to the bed and tortured her for hours before he'd finally let her come. Hmm. Yeah. She wouldn't mind something like that again.

He could obviously see that something naughty was going through her head because his smile had turned into a smirk, and when she met his gaze again he gave her a "If you don't stop looking at me like that right now, I'm going to drag you off and do wicked things to you" look. She was tempted to mouth, "Go on then," but it was only eleven o'clock and unfortunately they had several workshops to get through before they were done.

In the end, though, the day went quickly. They joined the others for lunch, and she got talking to a woman called Poppy who ran a bridal business in Wellington. As well as organizing the big day, Poppy sold wedding dresses and all the clothing associated with it, and she told Neve that she would be interested in looking at the Four Seasons catalogue to see if any of the lingerie would be suitable for her shop. Neve was able to tell her about the Snow White range that Rowan was in the process of designing inspired by her recent visit to Sweden with her partner, Hitch, when he went there to photograph reindeer for a commission. The new range featured beautiful white and silver embroidery on a variety of bras, panties, and all-in-ones that could easily double as bridal wear. They exchanged business cards and promised to contact each other on return to Wellington, so Neve was able to come away not only with a heap of marketing advice but a possible new business outlet.

The afternoon was spent in much the same way, with more workshops and different speakers offering their advice and suggestions for other marketing options. By the end of the day, Neve had a dozen ideas she was dying to try out, a handful of business contacts to keep in touch with, and some renewed enthusiasm, which she'd been starting to wonder if she'd ever feel again.

The day concluded with a round-up talk by Lisa that brought together everything they'd covered over the last few days. At the end, she encouraged everyone who was staying the final night to join them in the main hall for the midwinter party. Of course, Neve thought—it was the shortest day—the winter solstice. She'd forgotten that.

Although her parents were Catholic, she'd never felt much affinity with the religion and had stopped going to church as soon as she could get away with it. Her father hadn't been too pleased about it, but he'd realized that short of physically dragging her there every Sunday there was little he could do about it and had contented himself with carrying out sermons and lectures in his own time.

Because of the way her father was, she'd shied away from being interested in any other religion, but she did feel a connection with those who celebrated nature—the cycles of the Moon, the seasons, and the idea that—as could be seen in plants and trees—birth was followed by growth and then death and then rebirth. Midwinter marked the time when nature was moving into hibernation, sleeping for the cold months, only to reawaken in spring. She liked marking the seasons in that way, and found the idea of a midwinter party appealing, especially today, as a kind of celebration of Scott's passing.

So it was with some excitement that she went up to her room to rest and then change. She hadn't seen much of Rhett that afternoon as he'd been busy with other groups, but the idea of returning to her room with him later for a last session of hot sex shimmered in the air around her like the snow outside. She pushed away the sadness that also hovered at the notion that this would be the last time they'd sleep together. Tonight was for celebrating, and tomorrow would be a new beginning.

Her outfit hung on the wardrobe door, glistening as she walked in. She fingered the fabric, chewing her bottom lip. It had been an impulse buy, so different to anything else in her wardrobe that she couldn't believe it was hers. She hadn't even told her friends she'd bought it, because she'd known they'd tease her terribly. She could hear Callie's voice now—*Sequins, Neve? Are you coming down with a fever?* It wasn't her at all.

But for some reason, when she'd looked for something to wear to the midwinter party, she'd been unable to tear her gaze away from it. It was gorgeous and outrageous.

And if it didn't make Rhett's eyes pop out, nothing would.

Chapter Twenty-Two

Nowadays, Rhett didn't have a lot of time for parties, especially themed ones. He had no interest in dressing up as a vicar—or a tart for that matter—or as a gangster, or anything else they could come up with. Although he'd been to a lot of parties in his youth, now he was heading toward thirty he preferred the company of a small group of friends to the noise and hubbub of a large gathering.

Tonight was slightly different, though. There was no set costume—the only thing the organizers had suggested was that everyone wear something to symbolize the midwinter solstice, whether that was a red item of clothing, a bit of greenery, or something else festive to join in the fun.

And of course Neve was going to be there. It was his last chance to convince her that the two of them were meant to be together. It was a tall order, he knew. He'd hoped to have more time with her during the day, but at lunch she'd ended up talking to the bridal shop owner, and every other minute had been packed with work, so they'd had no time to talk.

Trying to stifle the feeling of despair that threatened to overwhelm him, he pulled on his favorite jeans and a black sweater over a white T-shirt, and pulled on the hat he'd chosen, wondering what Neve would be wearing. She wasn't a big fan of dressing up either—although he did remember a distinctly saucy nurse's uniform she'd acquired once…

Smiling, at just after seven, he went downstairs. He could hear the music as he walked across the foyer. They'd opted for a real band, and they were currently playing Stevie Wonder's *Superstition*, making him hum and move to the music even before he entered the hall.

He knew that the majority of the conference attendees had decided to stay on for the last night, and the place was already pleasantly busy. Tables full of finger food lined the walls with plenty of chairs for people who'd rather sit and talk or watch those dancing on the wooden floor in front of the flashing lights. Most of those already on the dance floor were women, but he knew the guys would venture up there after a few beers gave them a bit of Dutch courage. The table bore centerpieces of holly and ivy woven around tea lights, and at the back of the hall they'd projected the constellation of Matariki, also known as Pleiades or the Seven Sisters, to illustrate the Maori side of the festival.

He spotted Neve immediately, and although he'd thought it was artistic license and never actually happened in real life, he actually stopped walking and did a double take.

He wouldn't have called her a tomboy as such, but she wasn't a girly girl. She wore makeup and liked sexy lingerie, but the only time he'd ever seen her in a dress was the bridesmaid's one she'd worn to Willow's wedding.

Tonight, though, she looked absolutely stunning in a figure-hugging little black dress. It was extremely short and barely covered her butt, but had long sleeves—perfect for winter—and clung beautifully to her generous curves. Above her breasts, the dress featured a piece of net in a triangle shape that went from a point just above the outside of her right breast to the top of her left shoulder, outlined in sequins. It was sophisticated and sexy at the same time, and the sheer black tights and sexy black heels she wore with it were perfect.

She wore her dark hair loose but had pinned a large piece of glittery scarlet tinsel above her right ear as a concession to the solstice.

Glancing at the doorway, she spotted him standing there, staring at her. He saw her inhale, her eyes widen, and pleasure rippled through him that he still had that effect on her the same way she did him.

Carrying a wine glass, she skirted the dance floor and walked up to him.

"Evening," she said.

"Hey." She'd outlined her eyes tonight with black kohl and put something glittery on the lids. Jesus, she was sexy. He wasn't sure if he could wait until the end of the evening to get her back to his room.

"Nice antlers," she said.

He grinned. The festive hat had made him laugh when he saw it. "Glad you approve."

She glanced down at herself. "Do you like?"

In reply, he pressed the remote he'd slipped into his pocket. The red bulbs in the antlers flashed, and the right antler waved at her.

She burst out laughing. "Classy."

"I thought so." He slipped a hand onto her hip and smoothed it up her waist. "You look stunning."

"Thank you."

"Why do you always wear trousers? Your legs are amazing."

She said nothing, and he thought maybe his comment had flustered her.

"Every guy here is wishing you were going back to his room tonight," he murmured, lowering his lips until they almost touched hers and letting his hand warm the base of her spine, not quite resting on her butt.

"Hmm." She fluttered her long black eyelashes at him. "There'll only be one successful contestant though. I wonder who that will be?"

His heart rate picked up. It looked as if she was hoping the evening would end the same way he was. That, at least, boded well.

"Come and get a drink," she said, taking his hand, and she led him toward the bar.

*

Although he'd half dreaded the party, a couple of hours later Rhett had to admit to himself that he was having a good time.

The food was great—not too fancy for the average Kiwi guy but tasty and lots of it—and after a few plates and then a couple of beers to wash it down, he gave the hat to one of the kids staying at the hotel and was ready to take to the dance floor and show off his moves.

He and Neve had danced a lot when they were younger. Both of them had good rhythm, and they both enjoyed dancing, especially together. Tonight, in the little black dress, she looked spectacular, and he knew he wasn't the only one who couldn't keep his eyes off her as she wound her hips and bounced to the beat.

He'd wondered whether she'd want to dance with other guys, whether she'd act cool with him and keep him at arm's length, but she didn't leave his side, and the couple of times he saw another man ask her to dance, she smiled and said thanks but no thanks because she was with someone.

He mused on that as the evening wore on. He knew the news that Scott had passed away had shocked her that morning, and he'd hoped it might make her think about how short life was, and how it was best not to bear grudges and take each day as it came. Had she considered that? Certainly, she seemed in good spirits and was making it clear that she was interested in coming back to his room that night. He'd have to wait and see whether she wanted to continue to see him when they returned to Wellington.

The evening wore on, and in spite of the freezing weather outside the hall turned warm. Soon jackets were removed and sleeves rolled back as everyone relaxed and enjoyed themselves.

They'd left the huge red curtains tied back so everyone could see the snow falling outside, and to Rhett it felt as if they were encased in a giant snow globe, isolated from the rest of the world. He couldn't take his eyes from Neve with her shiny dark hair and her curves in all the right places, and he felt his blood heating throughout the evening as she danced before him, sexy and provocative in the short black dress.

His lustful state didn't improve when she leaned across him to pick up her glass of brandy at one point and whispered, "I've had an idea."

Distracted by the piece of net on her dress that gave him enticing flashes of the top of her breasts as she bent forward, he said, "Oh yeah?"

"Mmm." Her breath warmed his ear, giving him a hard-on in seconds. "Do you remember Kate's twenty-first?"

He certainly did. He hadn't known her friend well but he'd gone to the party as Neve's plus one. The party itself had been average, but much like tonight he'd had the hots for Neve all evening. Aware of that, she'd taunted him for hours with brushes of her boobs every time she leaned across him until he was practically exploding with lust, and then she'd—purposefully he was sure—been cheeky and given him some sass when he'd asked her a question in front of his mates. He couldn't remember what it was now, but his mates had all whistled and laughed, and Rhett had narrowed his eyes and promised himself that he'd make her pay for that later. And he had. He'd tied her to the bed with her tights and made love to her for hours, on and off, until—like the night before—she'd finally begged him to let her come.

"I remember," he said, trying to act cool, which was difficult with an erection the size of the Sky Tower.

"I thought I might return the favor," she said, her eyes dancing.

"Yeah, right. You'll have to catch me first."

"Maybe we'll wrestle for it. See who wins." Her eyes glittered. She wanted to fight him, and she wanted him to 'encourage' her to submit.

"Just say when," he murmured, brushing his lips against hers. "I'm happy to pretend to let you win for a little while."

Her lips curved up and she danced away, buoyed up by the music, laughing and winding her hips provocatively to entice him to follow her. So he did, and he pulled her into his arms so she bumped against him, every touch making him burn.

They danced for what seemed like hours, interspersing it with brief trips to the bar to refresh themselves before returning to the dance floor again, stopping only for the twenty minutes that the band requested for a break.

While they waited for them to return, they followed some of the others through the doors that had been thrown open temporarily to bring a bit of fresh air into the hall. Outside, it was dark and snowing heavily. Hopefully the airport would be clear enough for the plane to take off the next morning, he thought, shoving his hands in his pockets and shivering as they walked along the path.

"I don't think we'll stay out here long." Neve's teeth chattered as she picked her way carefully through the snow in her high heels, leading him away from the others.

He raised an eyebrow. "Are you cold or just pleased to see me?"

She glanced down and saw her nipples protruding through the black fabric like buttons and gave him a wry smile. "Cheeky."

He caught her by the hips and pressed her up against the wall. "You look magnificent in this dress." She shivered, and he groaned and nuzzled her neck. "Every time you shiver like that my trousers get tight."

She giggled and turned her head to let his lips brush hers. "Can I check?"

He chuckled. "I'm not going to let you grope me in public. I haven't had that much to drink." He was tempted, though. Tiny flakes of snow landed on her hair, her face, even her lashes. One landed on her lip, and she automatically touched her tongue to it, making him give a soft groan.

"Goodness," an amused voice said from behind them, "get a room you two."

Neve grinned at Lisa, who was walking back to the hall. "Don't worry, that's all in hand."

She laughed. "The two of you look very happy together. I'm glad you hooked up again."

"Yeah," he said. "It's been great."

"Wish I had a boy toy to take with me to conferences," Lisa said, giving Neve a wink. "Make the most of it." She scurried inside, shivering.

Neve pushed off the wall, ready to walk after her, but Rhett put an arm across her, stopping her passing.

"What did she mean by that?" he asked.

Neve wrinkled her nose. "I might have called you my boy toy. Sorry about that. I didn't think you'd mind."

"I don't," he said, because he didn't, particularly. It was the phrase *Make the most of it* that had attracted his attention.

"I just said it was fun having someone to play with while I was away," Neve said. "She asked how we knew each other, and I explained that we were an item once and were having a fling. I think she rather liked the idea of having a plaything too." She chuckled and then shivered again. "Come on, I'm freezing."

He didn't move. She walked a few steps then realized he wasn't following her and stopped.

"What?" she asked. Her cool blue eyes were wide, innocent. She wasn't teasing him. She genuinely believed that once they returned to Wellington, that would be it—they would be done.

"Nothing," he said.

She shrugged and hurried back into the hall.

Rhett watched her go, his mind whirling like the flurries of flakes outside.

Chapter Twenty-Three

Neve hadn't slept much the night before, and although she was having a good time, her energy was waning, and she wanted to make sure she had enough left for whatever lay ahead. Her pulse racing, she finished off her drink and leaned toward Rhett.

"Well," she whispered in his ear. "Shall we?"

She moved back and shivered a little as he considered her words. His eyes were cautious, cool. She thought she might have upset him by calling him her boy toy, although he'd said she hadn't, and it had only been in fun.

Even as doubt flickered through her, though, he smiled and said, "Sure."

She blew out a sigh of relief and held out her hand. He took it and let her lead him from the room.

In the foyer, it was cooler, and she shivered as they walked across to the elevators. She pressed the button, and they waited for the carriage to descend.

"Are you okay?" she asked him, unnerved by his silence. He just nodded. "Are you angry with me?" She tried to sound irritated but was aware that it came out a little pathetic. "If you don't want to tonight, for God's sake, just say so."

The doors dinged behind her and opened. Rhett walked forward, forcing her to move backward into the carriage. He pressed the button for his floor as he passed it but continued walking forward until she met the wall with a bump. She caught her breath, startled, and watched the doors closed behind him.

"Rhett..." she whispered, not quite able to read his mood. She was certain he was cross with her, but as he moved up against her and pressed his hips to hers, she felt his erection thick and hard against her mound and realized he couldn't be that mad.

He moved his arms around her, and as the carriage shuddered and lifted, he lowered his lips to hers and kissed her. She closed her eyes, concentrating on the way he sent a tingle through her whole body, and gave a little moan as his tongue dipped into her mouth.

What she hadn't realized was that it was a diversionary tactic. Behind her back, he'd obviously been searching for the zipper of her dress, because suddenly he tugged it down from the nape of her neck to her tailbone, and the stretchy fabric released its tight hold on her skin and slid off her shoulders.

"Rhett!" She gasped and caught the dress, clutching hold of it as he grasped the hem and tugged. "Stop it!"

He ignored her and tugged harder, but she had too tight a hold on it. He changed tactics and lifted it, peeling it up her body, and she shrieked as she felt it pass over her hips and waist.

She tried to back away to the corner of the carriage, but there was no escape. She'd forgotten how strong he was, and he pinned her there, and then his mouth was on hers again as he caught her hands and tried to peel them away from the dress.

"Get off!" If she was in his room, she might have let him do it, but they were in the elevator for Christ's sake and there was every possibility that when the doors opened someone might be waiting outside.

He didn't seem to care and appeared determined to have her naked. She groaned as he delved his tongue deep into her mouth, firing her up on all cylinders, turning her on with his sheer strength and power.

Finally, he caught both her hands in one of his and held them above her head, then grasped her dress and tugged it down over her breasts.

Panicking now that she really was going to end up naked, she twisted out of his grasp and ducked under his arm to the other side of the carriage as she tried to cover herself. He was on her in seconds, but at that moment the carriage rocked to a halt and the doors opened.

She pushed him away and ran out, relieved beyond belief to find the corridor empty, the majority of the guests presumably at the party. Rhett advanced on her quickly, though, and before she could stop him, he bent and grabbed her in a fireman's lift, hefting her up over his shoulder so her head and arms dangled down his back.

She shrieked. "Rhett!"

He smacked her behind, hard, as he marched forward. "Stop squealing. You'll wake the guests."

"Put me down!" She kicked, but he put an arm across her calves as strong as an iron bar, and even though she hammered her fists on his back, all he did was laugh.

"Shit." She gave in and went limp, knowing he wouldn't release her until they were in his room.

Upside down, she watched the doors go by until he stopped, swiped the card, and opened one. He carried her inside, and she saw the door swing shut behind her. He continued moving into the dark room and paused in front of the bed.

Neve's mouth went dry, and her heart raced. His eyes had lit up when she'd mentioned the last time he'd tied her down, and she half hoped, half feared that he'd do it again. Maybe she shouldn't have mentioned it. He seemed in a strange mood, and they'd been apart for so long that she wasn't sure how it would affect him.

He wouldn't hurt her—she was sure of that. He might have been rough and forceful, but the one time—the last time—she'd fought him, as soon as he'd realized she wasn't playing he'd backed off immediately.

That didn't mean he wouldn't try to beat his previous record and torture her for hours though. She'd wanted him to when she'd suggested it, but now they were there, she felt oddly nervous.

"Put me down," she demanded.

He smacked her butt again. "Stop ordering me around."

"I'll do what I fucking like."

"Don't you always." He lowered her then, but to her surprise hefted her forward unceremoniously so that she fell onto her back on the bed with enough force to make her bounce all over the place.

"Hey." She rolled onto her front and tried to crawl away, but he caught her ankle and dragged her back to him.

Catching her dress by the hem, he tugged it up, catching her unawares. She squealed and rolled onto her back to fight him but only succeeded in making it easier for him to raise her arms and pull it up over her head.

Speechless at how quickly he'd stripped her, she pushed his hands away as he caught her tights at the waist and yanked them down over her hips. She was no match for him, though, and within seconds her legs were bare and he was sitting astride her.

Determined not to be the only one naked on the bed, she held the base of his sweater and pulled it up. He let her tug it off his head, and she started on the buttons of his shirt.

She'd almost reached the bottom when he took her tights in both hands and ripped the two halves apart in one easy yank. She inhaled sharply and stared at him, her heart rate doubling in speed at the wicked gleam in his eyes.

She moistened her lips. "Fuck."

He tipped his head to the side. "All in good time."

Neve's heart hammered. The butterflies in her stomach wouldn't go away, and her breathing quickened as he braced his hands either side of her shoulders and looked down at her.

"Rhett..." she said nervously.

"What?" He caught her hands and held them above her head, then bent and brushed his lips along her cheek. "Isn't this what you want, sweetheart? To be conquered? To be tamed?"

"No." She was nearly panting now.

He gave a soft laugh. "Yeah, right." He pressed his lips to her neck, and she felt his tongue touch her skin, tasting, teasing, all the way up to her ear. He sucked the lobe, then breathed softly, making her shiver. "You want me," he whispered. "Say it."

Irritable at his smug tone, she shook her head.

She should have known that would have repercussions. He kissed down her neck, then fastened his mouth there and sucked. She squealed and bucked beneath him, but it was like trying to throw off a grizzly bear.

He lowered on top of her, his weight pressing her into the mattress, and stayed there until she stopped struggling and glared at him. His eyes burned into hers, unforgiving, and yet full of emotion too. What was it? Tenderness? Sadness? Why was he sad?

Forgetting their game for a moment, she lifted her head to touch her lips to his. To her surprise, though, he moved his lips out of her reach. She tried again, and again he moved back. His eyes glinted in the lamplight.

Rearing up, he caught her by the waist and pulled her easily a few feet up the bed so her head was on the pillows. Then he caught her right hand and reached for one of the legs of her tights that he'd ripped.

"Rhett..."

He ignored her and looped it around her wrist, and had soon secured it to one of the slats in the headboard. With one hand tied she was no match for him, and within moments he'd tied the other one too.

Her heart hammered. What did he have planned? What was he going to do to her?

He leaned over her and lowered his head, his lips just above hers, his breath warming them. He stayed like that for a long moment. Both of them were breathing heavily, and she swallowed hard, almost trembling with anticipation.

Then, to her surprise, he rose and got off the bed. He lifted his hands to his shirt, and she waited for him to undo the final buttons and shoulder it off.

To her surprise, he began to button it up.

She blinked a few times. "Rhett?"

He turned away and picked up his sweater. Then he turned back to her. This time, his eyes were hard, cold as he studied her.

Neve couldn't catch her breath. She stared at him, suddenly realizing that something was terribly wrong.

"Rhett?" Anger rushed through her as he surveyed her coolly. "Untie me."

He tossed the sweater onto the bed. "No."

"What the hell?" She yanked at her wrists, but they were tied too securely.

"Maybe now you'll listen to me." He moved closer to the bed. Furious, she lashed out a foot, but he was just out of reach. "Enough, Neve," he snapped. "You're going to listen until I'm finished, and then you're going to think about what I've said for a while."

"What the fuck are you talking about?"

"Shut up!" he yelled. Then he sank his hands into his hair. "What the hell do you do to me? I haven't shouted at anyone for years!"

"And there's me thinking you've changed," she said sarcastically.

"I have changed," he snapped.

"Nobody changes," she bit back, "not really."

"Yes. They do. It's possible for everyone to change—except you and your fucking father."

She glared at him. "What do you mean?"

"I mean that both of you are too fucking stubborn to admit you're wrong."

"Wrong about what?"

"About us! You were wrong before, and you're wrong now."

"Oh, and you know everything, Mr. Fucking Perfect, and I just have to sit here and—"

"Enough," he said, hard enough to make her stop in her tracks. "This time, I'm doing the talking, and you're going to listen, or do you want me to gag you?"

She stared at him. "You wouldn't."

"Wouldn't I?"

Normally, she would have said no way would he have done something like that to her—that it was an idle threat. At that moment, though, she wasn't so sure. His eyes blazed, and he looked as if he was having trouble holding himself back from strangling her.

"Go on then," she said irritably. "Say what you have to say."

He put his hands on his hips, and his chest heaved. "I love you."

That she hadn't expected. Her jaw dropped.

"I love you," he said again, this time with a touch of surprise, as if he'd only just realized himself. "I loved you back then, and I don't think I've stopped loving you over the last five years. I'm crazy about you. Or you make me crazy—I'm not sure which." He ran his hand through his hair again.

Too dumbfounded, she could only stare at him, her head spinning.

"We could be great together," he continued. "But you just won't let it happen, will you? You're stuck in the past, and nothing I can say will drag you out of it."

"You made the decision to join the squad without me," she began, not willing to take all the blame, but he dismissed it with a wave of his hand.

"Yes, I did, and I was wrong to do that. I admit it now."

"It doesn't matter. You broke my heart, and I can't forgive that." Her voice caught.

He didn't come to console her, though. "I know, and that's what's so terribly sad. People make mistakes, Neve. Like your father. He said something dumb because he has a picture in his mind of what the perfect daughter is like, and you broke it. He was stupid and idiotic, and he's too proud to say so."

"So it's up to me to take the step?" she asked, aghast. "After what he said?"

"I don't know. I don't have all the answers, but I do know that if you don't try, you'll never speak to your father again. Is that what you want? Do you want to get a phone call from your mother or your sister one day to say he's passed away, and you never had a chance to make up with him?"

She was nearly losing it now, torn between fury, frustration, and misery. "Let me go," she half sobbed, half screamed. "You can't keep me tied up like this."

"I'm not done yet. I've waited for you, Neve. I didn't realize it until now, but I have waited for you all these years. I was so sure that once you understood how good we'd had it, you'd come around and forgive me, and we could move forward again. I don't mean in a relationship, I just mean as friends. I was ecstatic when you sat with me and had breakfast the other morning. What happened between us occurred because we are so right for one another. But you're like a fucking saboteur—you're fucking Guy Fawkes blowing up the Houses of Parliament. You're determined to destroy everything good in your life because you're so damn stubborn. You have such high standards—you set the bar up here." He gestured above his head. "It's no wonder that everyone fails to reach it—including you."

"Let me go!"

"We only have one life. One chance at it. Look at what happened to Scott, for fuck's sake. Look at what happened to me! It can happen to anyone at any moment. We don't know when our time's up. We need to make the most of every opportunity and stop holding grudges. When I was sick, I read that you should start every day afresh and put all hurt and resentment behind you. It's amazing how you can feel when you do that. When you wake up in the morning and it really is a brand new day."

She wrenched at her hands. "Rhett!"

"People make mistakes. Including you. Adults realize this, and adults can forgive each other when they do it. When we were twenty-one, we were still children at heart, but you're not twenty-one now, Neve, you're twenty-seven. You need to stop being a fucking child and grow up."

"Let me go!" she screaming. "I fucking hate you! Let me go."

He picked up his sweater. "Take some time to think about what I've said. The ties aren't tight. When you calm down, you'll realize you can easily get out of them. When you do, I'll be in the bar if you want to talk. Otherwise, have a nice flight tomorrow."

To her shock, horror, and fury, he turned, walked out of the room, and let the door shut behind him.

Chapter Twenty-Four

Rhett was sure that Neve was going to scream the place down, and he half prepared himself for someone to come running out of the adjoining bedroom, ready to ring the manager, or even the police. At that moment, though, he didn't care. He walked away, took the stairs, and went down to the ground floor. Ignoring the hall, he slipped into the quiet bar, ordered himself a whisky, and sat on a stool.

His heart banged against his ribs for about ten minutes. He repeatedly glanced at the door, expecting her to march in ready to smash a chair over his head, and his brain churned through replies for the accusations he knew she'd throw at him, preparing an argument for the case she'd make against him.

As the minutes ticked by, though, gradually his heart slowed, and a sick feeling began to appear in his stomach. She wasn't coming down. She'd either gone back to her room, or she could have even left the building, just walked out.

He leaned his elbows on the bar and sank his hands into his hair. *You fucking idiot.* The full realization of what he'd done began to sink in.

He'd once read of a red mist that descended on soldiers on the battlefield, and he felt as if he'd experienced something similar that was only just beginning to clear. When Lisa had said *Make the most of it*, and Neve had admitted she only wanted him for the night, fury had swept over him. He knew she loved him. He'd seen it in her eyes, heard it in her sighs, and the way she reacted to him told him her feelings for him—like his for her—hadn't changed since they'd broken up. But her stubbornness had gotten in the way. And now, even though she'd learned that he'd been ill, and even though that should have shocked her into realizing how she felt for him, she still couldn't let the scab heal over. She had to keep picking at it, drawing fresh blood every time.

He blew out a long breath, tears pricking his eyes. And now she would never talk to him again. At least if she'd come down and thrown something at him, screamed at him, he'd have had some reaction. But this... This was worse. This meant she'd truly cut him out of her life.

Unless... An icy feeling slid down his spine. Unless she really couldn't get out of the ties. No, he'd made sure that once she looked at them carefully, she'd see how easy it was to slip her hands out. But maybe she was too angry or too upset to do that. Maybe she was still there, growing more and more angry or upset. He couldn't leave her there. He was going to have to go back up and check.

He'd wait another five minutes, and then he'd go and find out.

The hand on the clock ticked around so slowly he thought it might be broken. But eventually five minutes passed, and she didn't appear.

"Fuck." He finished off the whisky in one gulp, slammed the glass on the bar, and left.

He walked up the stairs, conscious that she might at that moment be taking the elevator down, hoping she was, dreading she wasn't. With feet like lead, he walked back along the corridor to his room, swiped his keycard, and gingerly opened the door.

The room was empty. The ripped tights were still looped around the headboard, but Neve had gone.

He inhaled deeply, although he wasn't sure if it was from relief or disappointment. That meant she'd made the decision not to come and talk to him. She wasn't just angry—she must be apoplectic with rage.

He sat on the edge of the bed and ran a hand through his hair. Sorrow swept over him. He'd lost her. He'd had her within reach, like a man stretching across a chasm to grab a ladder, and he'd missed it and fallen. He'd never get her back now.

Outside, snow was still falling, and he looked out and watched it fluttering down, so incredibly beautiful, and yet he could find no pleasure in it now.

Then his gaze fell on something. The room had a small balcony, and in the corner on the floor was a dark shape, almost invisible against the darker night. As he watched, though, it moved, and his heart leapt.

He rose and walked over to the sliding door and pulled it slowly open. She twitched at the sound but didn't look up. Instead, she turned her face away. She sat right in the corner, her knees drawn up, and she rested her cheek on them, her arms around her legs, hugging them tight. His heart broke as he saw that she was wearing one of his sweaters, although her legs and feet were bare.

"Neve." He rushed over to her and dropped to his haunches beside her. "What the fuck are you doing out here? You're going to freeze to death."

She was shivering, but she didn't move. Snow lay on the edge of the balustrade and the small round table and chairs, and flakes were beginning to land on her arms.

Carefully, he lowered himself down onto the tiles beside her. In the past, she'd hated to be touched when she was upset. She wasn't one of those women who liked to be molly coddled.

"Neve?" he said softly. "Come on, honey. Let's go inside. It's freezing out here."

She shook her head and said something, the words muffled against the sweater.

"Hmm? What did you say?"

She turned her face a little. "I fucked up."

He frowned. "What do you mean?"

"Some people never find him, and I found him, and then I lost him."

"Neve, what are you talking about sweetheart? Found who?"

"Mr. Right. My soul mate. I found you, and then I fucked it up, and now I've lost you."

Emotion washed over him, and suddenly he felt full of regret for what he'd done to her. He'd thought her so hard that he had to break through the layer of ice surrounding her, but now he realized how thin that layer had been.

"Hey, you haven't lost me. I'm right here, aren't I?"

"I've been so stupid," she said as if she hadn't heard him. "It's all my fault."

She'd never wanted comforting in the past, but suddenly he remembered how she'd come up to him when she'd heard that he'd had cancer, and how she'd put her arms around him. Maybe she'd changed too, and neither of them had realized.

He lowered an arm around her shoulders. She didn't curl up to him, but she didn't push him away either. He took that as a good sign.

"It's not all your fault," he said. "Of course it's not. I was an idiot. I should have consulted you before I agreed to take that place on the team. I should have considered your feelings, and we should have talked about it together. We were a couple, weren't we? It wasn't my decision to make alone. I know that now. At the time I didn't realize what I'd done. I was young and arrogant, and all I could think about was how excited I was. I thought you were just jealous. Now I'm older and wiser, sort of, I know better. I was wrong, and I'm sorry."

She turned her cool blue eyes up to him and stared at him. And then she covered her face with her hands and started to cry.

She'd never done that before. The fact that she was crying shook him up more than anything else could have done. She'd only ever cried once when she was with him, and that was right at the end, and mostly out of frustration.

"Hey." That was it—he wasn't going to sit out here any longer, not when she was feeling bad enough to cry.

He got to his feet, bent and slid his arms under her, and lifted her up. To his relief, she didn't fight him, just curled against him. He carried her inside and shut the door behind him, and took her over to the bed.

After pulling back the duvet, he placed her on the mattress and covered her over. He flicked on the electric blanket because her legs were icy, and she needed warming up. Then he piled the pillows up and sat back on them, gathered her into his arms, and tucked the duvet around her. The blanket was already warming up. While he waited, he rubbed her arms and back, kissing her hair and murmuring to her.

"Come on," he whispered, holding her tightly. "You're breaking my heart. Don't cry, sweetheart. I'm so sorry I tied you up—I shouldn't have. I was angry that you were talking about our time here as temporary, and frustrated that you wouldn't admit that you like being with me. I want to start dating you again when we go back to Wellington. I can't live without you. I love you, can't you see that?"

Unfortunately, that only served to make her cry more. Rhett looked up at the ceiling and decided to keep his mouth shut for a while. Clearly, he had no idea how to say the right thing.

For about ten minutes she sniffled and snuffled, and then finally, as the bed began to warm, she calmed. He pulled a couple of tissues from the box beside the bed and gave them to her, and she blew her nose and wiped her face, then cuddled up to him again.

"Can I get you anything?" he murmured. "A drink? Something to eat?"

She shook her head. "I'm okay."

At last, she was talking to him. He moved back a little to look at her. She didn't meet his gaze but studied his chest, reaching out a hand to trace a finger along the V-neck of his sweater. Her eyes were red and her makeup had run, but she was still the most beautiful woman he'd ever seen.

"Are you?" he asked. "Okay?"

She gave a small nod. "I'm sorry about that."

"You have nothing to apologize for. I have everything. I shouldn't have done that, sweetheart. I was angry and frustrated, but I had no right to tie you up and leave you. I regret it, and I wish I could go back in time and not have done it. I'm such an idiot."

"So you haven't changed that much," she joked weakly.

"No." He smiled. "Obviously not." He cupped her chin and lifted it so she looked into his eyes. "Forgive me?" he pleaded.

She nodded. "Maybe we should start again tomorrow. I like what you said about that. I'm going to try to do that. Start each day afresh."

"It's not easy to let go of all the pain and anger, but it is possible. It helps to accept that other people make mistakes, too. It makes us a bigger person if we can give them a chance to say they're sorry and to make amends. If they don't, well, we've tried, and we've nothing to blame ourselves for."

"When did you get so old and wise?" she teased.

"Well obviously, I still make mistakes."

"You have changed though. I was envious of you, Rhett. I felt as if I'd walked into wet concrete and my feet had stuck in the past. I couldn't move forward. Every time I thought about what had happened between us, I couldn't get rid of the feelings it stirred up."

"And now? Do you think you can move on?"

"You still want to?" Her voice was little more than a whisper.

"I do. More than anything."

She swallowed. "I'll try. I can't promise anything, Rhett, but I'll try."

His throat tightened. He'd just tied her up and walked out on her, and here she was giving him hope for the future.

"I'm sorry," he said. "For hurting you. For everything bad I've done."

"I know. In an odd way, I think I needed something like that to jerk the train off the rails, you know?" Her look turned wry. "I'm not saying I think you should do it again if we argue."

"*When* we argue." He kissed her nose. "I always loved arguing with you because I loved making up. But I won't ever do anything like that to you again. I promise I'll do my best never to hurt you as long as I live."

Chapter Twenty-Five

Tears pricked Neve's eyes again, and she swallowed hard to try to stop them falling. She'd cried more in the last thirty minutes than she had over the last five years—she couldn't start again.

Rhett's face held such tenderness, though, such love, that it was impossible to hold them back.

"Aw." He brushed a thumb across her cheek. "You're a softie deep down, aren't you?"

She didn't know how she could have gone from the depths of despair to such happiness within the space of minutes. Up until an hour ago, she'd convinced herself she had no plans to get back with him again, but when he'd walked out of the room leaving her tied to the bed, she'd realized it was the nail in the coffin of their relationship, and it had shocked her to the core. Only then had she understood the depths of her feelings for him, and the thought that she'd ruined it forever had made everything tumble down around her ears.

But he'd come back, and he'd taken her in his arms, and he'd said he was sorry. Just those simple words had been enough to break her. He hadn't denied that he'd hurt her, or insisted he was right. He'd said he'd made a mistake, and it was time to acknowledge that and move on.

You should start every day afresh and put all hurt and resentment behind you. She still wasn't a hundred percent certain she could do that, but she was going to try.

He'd been looking into her eyes for a while and, maybe seeing her feelings for him reflected in them, he smiled and lowered his lips to hers. Gently, tentatively, giving her the option to move back if it wasn't what she wanted.

It was, though, and she closed her eyes and welcomed the kiss. His lips moved across hers tenderly, and she raised her hand to slip into his hair as she opened her mouth to his tongue.

Man, he knew how to kiss. He knew exactly the right pressure to use, and he understood how a brush of lips or a touch of his tongue was enough to send skitters up her spine and her nipples tightening in her bra. It was lovely lying there, the heat of the electric blanket soaking into her limbs, safe and secure in the circle of his arms, just kissing, letting her emotions settle like the snowflakes outside.

When he finally lifted his head to survey her, as if making sure she was enjoying it, she whispered, "Will you get into bed with me?"

He hesitated. "We don't have to…"

"I know."

His lips curved up. "Okay."

He rose from the bed, and she hugged the pillow and watched him undress. He didn't exactly do a striptease, but he did take off his clothes slowly, keeping his gaze on her. First he tugged off his black sweater, and he dropped it onto the chair, running a hand through his hair where the sweater had made it stick up. Then he unbuttoned his shirt, taking his time, before letting it slip from his shoulders and tossing it onto the chair too.

Next, he toed off his shoes, undid his belt, and unbuttoned his trousers, and he slipped those off along with his socks, leaving him standing there in his dark-gray boxer briefs. His erection was already visible, and her heart picked up speed as he peeled his underwear over it.

"Sorry," he said, following her gaze as he climbed under the covers. "It has a mind of its own."

"Don't ever apologize for that."

He laughed and pulled her into his arms, and she rolled onto her back, bringing him with her so his weight pressed her into the mattress. He smoothed her hair back from her face, and she waited for him to kiss her, but instead he surveyed her, his eyes serious.

"I'm sorry I hurt you," he said. "Then and now."

"I'm sorry I've been so stubborn. We've wasted so much time. I still can't believe you were so sick." Her throat tightened, and she had to swallow down the lump that formed there. "I wish I could have been with you while you had your treatment. I'm sorry you had to go through it on your own."

He tucked a strand of hair behind her ear. "These things define us. I learned a lot about myself during that time. I grew up a lot. It made me a better person, I think."

"I've missed you."

He brushed his thumb across her lip. "I've missed you too."

"I tried to pretend I didn't, but I did."

He kissed her, just once, a soft press of his lips to hers.

She cupped his face and looked into his hazel eyes. "Do you really think we can make it work?"

"I can't tell what will happen in the future, or how we'll feel ten years from now. All I can say is that right here, right now, I don't ever want to let you go again. I want you in my arms for the rest of my life. If you think that's a bit over the top, I get it, and we'll just play it by ear and concentrate on each day as it comes. But I'm not going anywhere, and I want you to know that. Relationships aren't easy, and there'll be ups and downs, but I'm not going anywhere."

"You mean I'm stuck with you whether I like it or not?"

His lips curved up. "Yeah."

"Crap."

He chuckled and kissed her again. "I love you, Neve Clark."

She took a deep, shivery breath. "And I love you, Rhett Butler."

His expression turned wry. "I'm going to have to make you pay for that."

"I hoped you would."

He rolled and pulled her on top of him, smoothing his hands down her back and over her butt, then back up under the sweater to cup her breasts. Her body responded to him, as it always did, but her mind flew away out of the window and into the snowy night, spiraling up into the stars. Could they really make a go of it? Could she put aside the huge burden of resentment and grief she'd been carrying around with her for five years, pull back her shoulders, and finally walk tall? It seemed as huge a wish as asking to win the lottery.

"I love you," he murmured, kissing around to her ear.

Her eyes stung again. Jeez. How could he reduce her to tears with those simple words?

"I love you too," she said, realizing she hadn't said it back.

He stared at her for a moment, then sat up, pulling her with him. First, he removed her sweater, adding, "It looks better on you," before he tossed it to one side. Then he unclipped her bra, drew the straps down her arms, and that joined the sweater on the floor. Finally, he slid her panties down her legs and got rid of them too.

"Mmm," he said with approval, lying back and bringing her with him. "At last."

This time when he kissed her there was heat behind it, and Neve gladly gave herself over to him, letting him delve his tongue into her mouth and stroke his hands over her body. At one point she began kissing down his chest, but he gently pushed her away, and she understood that he wanted to concentrate on her and show her how he felt.

He disappeared under the covers, and she felt his lips brush down her neck to her breasts, where he teased her nipples with his lips and tongue for a while until she was groaning and clutching her hands in his hair. Trailing his lips down over her belly to between her legs, he sank his tongue into her folds. Neve closed her eyes and tilted her hips toward him, shuddering, startled to feel tears leaking from her eyes as he aroused her so tenderly.

It wasn't long before he kissed back up her body, but when he lay along her again and bent to kiss her lips, he moved back and frowned. "Are you okay?"

She nodded. "Just a bit… overwhelmed. I'll be all right."

He smoothed her hair back from her face and pressed his lips to her cheeks, her nose, her mouth. "Don't cry."

"I'm not. Not really. I can't help it. I'm sorry. I feel like I've been given a second chance, and I don't deserve it."

"Of course you do. Everyone makes mistakes, Neve. That's what you have to realize." He lifted up, reached for a condom, and rolled it on. Then he leaned back over her. "Turn over," he said.

She twisted onto her front, thinking that it would have been nice to have made love so she could look into his eyes and watch his face as he came, but as he settled on top of her and wrapped his arms around her, she discovered she didn't mind so much.

"I thought you were going to argue with me," he murmured as he slid inside her.

She rested her forehead on the pillow with a groan. "It's a temporary lapse. Make the most of it."

He chuckled and kissed her neck, her ear, and her mouth when she lifted it to him, and moved slowly, keeping close to her, warming her with his body.

"Will you stay with me?" His arms were tight, as if he was afraid to let her go. "Will you let me do this to you every night?"

She closed her eyes, loving the feel of him wrapped around her, heavy and hot. "Every night?" she whispered.

"As often as I can manage it. I can't get enough of you. I want you all the time. Your soft body drives me crazy. All I do is dream about the next time I can make love to you." He thrust rhythmically, sliding easily inside her.

"Mmm, Rhett..."

Slipping his hand underneath her, he teased her clit with a finger while he continued to move. She gasped, and he plunged his tongue into her mouth, sending her senses spinning as her body began to tighten.

"Come for me," he said, kissing her neck. She moaned, waiting for him to thrust harder, faster, but his hips kept up their slow pace, his finger stroking through her swollen flesh. It was almost as if he still held the remote control—he was so skilled at this, at controlling the pace of her arousal.

She loved this bit—the steady build, the anticipation, her body gradually tensing and reacting to him, pleasure intensifying, and the blissful, almost painful sensation as muscles deep inside contracted to send warmth and ecstasy spreading throughout her.

He stopped moving, letting her clamp around him as she cried out his name, murmuring how much he loved her as he kissed her, his tenderness and gentle touch almost making her weep again.

Only when her body had released her from the intense pulses did he begin to move again, still telling her he loved her, his voice husky with emotion, until his body also locked in blissful release, and he gasped her name too as he came.

When he finally relaxed, he withdrew, making her mumble a complaint, but within seconds he turned her to face him and wrapped her in his arms.

"This bed's like an oven," she grumbled. "I'm all hot and sweaty."

"Are you trying to turn me on?"

"Oh, stop it." She smacked his arm, then nestled into his embrace.

"You were freezing." He stroked her back. "I was worried you might get frostbite."

"I didn't even notice the cold."

He kissed her head. "It's surprising how emotional pain can be stronger than physical pain sometimes. I remember thinking that after my op. It hurt, but not as much as it hurt when we broke up."

Neve moved back a little to look into his eyes. "I wish I'd known. I thought you walked away and didn't look back."

He stroked her cheek. "I did nothing but look back. I didn't contact you because I didn't think you'd want to talk to me. As time passed and I missed you so much, I started to think about us getting back together. When I returned to Wellington, I had doubts that it would happen because you were obviously still so furious with me. I tried to tell myself it was definitely over, but something deep inside me wouldn't believe it."

She kissed his hand. "I'm glad you didn't give up."

"How could I, when we're meant to be together?" His eyes were serious, honest.

"You really think that, don't you?"

"Yes."

"You believe in soul mates?" She hadn't thought guys believed in stuff like that.

He looked amused. "I don't know if I'd have called it that. It sounds a bit New-Age-y. And I don't know if it's as simple as there's one person that exists in the world and you have to find him or her. I'm not saying there's something supernatural about it. All I know is that this feels right, and being apart from you felt wrong. And I don't want to be apart from you again."

"Aw. You're such a softie."

He smiled and took her hand in his. "There is something I have to ask you, though."

"Oh?"

"Well, an issue I feel I should raise. It's about having kids."

Her heart skipped a beat. "Oh."

"I can still have them, as far as I know. The op shouldn't have changed my fertility rate. And anyway, as I said, I banked some sperm at the time just in case. But it's not that. Scientists reckon that maybe one in four cases of testicular cancer is hereditary. My grandfather had it, and so did my father. I just…" He hesitated. "It might be something you need to think about. That if we had a son, he might inherit the gene." He stared at her. "Why are you smiling?"

"If we had a son?"

His lips curved up. "Yeah. Well, there's a fifty-fifty chance."

"You're really serious about this, aren't you?"

"I'm nearly thirty. I'm sure most men start thinking about settling down around that age anyway, and having cancer started me thinking about what I'd leave behind. I want a family. Not immediately, not until you're ready, but it's on my list."

Neve was seconds away from crying again. How was it possible for him to say so many nice things in such a short space of time?

"It doesn't matter to me," she said. "It means there's a three in four chance that he wouldn't have the gene, and even if he does, it doesn't mean he'd definitely get it, surely? I don't believe you shouldn't do things in life because there's a small chance of something going wrong. You said that you have to take opportunities as they come, and you were right." She sniffed hard, trying to keep the tears in. "What else is on your list?"

He shrugged. "Lots of things."

"Like what?"

"Neve, an hour ago you hated my guts. I don't know if I'm ready to put my whole heart on the table."

"Aw, come on."

He sighed. "Well, marriage, obviously. Probably before the kids bit."

Her heart skipped another beat. He laughed. "You look like I slapped you with a wet fish. What's surprising about that?"

"I thought you were going to say something about sex."

"Oh, that's on the list too, don't worry." He grinned, then cupped her face. "Don't get me wrong. We're in no rush. I want to date you properly for a while, to make sure that it's what you want too. I want to tell our friends about us, and see you every day, and maybe move in together eventually, and see what happens after that. We'll wait, if that's what you want. But, like I said, I'm not going anywhere."

"I love you," she said, and it felt good to say it, and right, because even though she'd tried to harden her heart against him, he'd always owned it. Why had she not understood that?

"I love you, too." He kissed her and pulled her into his arms.

She lay there for a while, drawing on his chest, conscious of the snow falling outside, blanketing the world in its white quietness. Thoughts whirled through her head, but she didn't try to analyze them or push them away. Instead, she studied each one as it passed through her mind and let them settle, trying to appreciate them for what they were rather than constantly telling herself what she should or ought to be feeling.

She thought he'd fallen asleep, but he must have been thinking and watching the snow too, because eventually he said, "Penny for them."

Lifting up, she propped her head on her hand. "I was thinking about my dad."

He faced her, adopting the same pose. "Are you going to see him again?"

She nodded. "I was thinking about what you said, about starting each day afresh, and accepting that people make mistakes. He hurt my feelings, and it's difficult to let that go, and I'm not sure he will apologize for what he said, but I'm trying to accept that it's not necessarily about trying to get rid of the things that have gone wrong."

"Yeah. It's kind of like finding a tree log that's fallen across the road. You don't just finish the journey because something's in the way. You either move it or, if it's too heavy, you leave it there and find a way around it. It'll always be there, in your rear-view mirror, but as you drive away, it'll get smaller and smaller until you can hardly see it at all."

She nodded. "That's a great analogy. I can't erase what he said, or those feelings he created, but maybe we can try to find a way to move on." She drew her brows together. "I'll try, anyway. I'm not sure I'll be cured overnight."

"Trying's all you can do, sweetheart. Why don't I come with you? We can tell your folks we're dating again—the news might smooth things over a bit."

Her dad had always liked Rhett, so it wasn't the worst idea in the world. "Okay."

"Now come here and try to get some sleep." He pulled her into his arms again. "You've got suitcases under your eyes and you look knackered."

"I'm knackered because someone's screwed me all the way into next week."

"Tell whoever did that to you that you need some rest, for crying out loud."

She laughed and snuggled up to him. "I will."

He kissed her hair. "Goodnight."

"'Night." And before she could say anything else, she fell asleep.

Chapter Twenty-Six

"So what's this news you've been dying to tell us?" Birdie asked. "Come on, out with it."

It was Friday evening, and as usual Neve's friends had gathered at the bar on Wellington quay for an end-of-the-week drink.

Callie was there with her husband Gene. Callie was six months' pregnant and told everyone she was as fat as an elephant and walking like one, although Neve thought she looked perfect—all glowy and satisfied, out of the 'throwing up' stage and not quite at the 'get it out of me' stage.

Rowan and her fiancé Hitch were there, catching up with everyone before they headed off to South America. Rowan's sister Willow was there too with her husband Liam and their son, who was now sixteen-months-old, a naughty little cherub currently sitting on Rowan's lap, playing with her iPad and swiping the pages of a children's book as if he'd used one all his life.

Birdie, the fourth member of the Four Seasons, was also there with her partner, Mal. She'd been going out with him for years but their relationship had been very on-off, with regular breakups and get-back-togethers, mainly because, so it seemed to Neve, he refused to commit. However, they'd finally set a date for their wedding of October 2, surprising everyone. Neve was pleased for her friend, although secretly she wasn't sure what Birdie saw in him, and thought she could have done better. She'd never liked the way he treated Birdie, and even though he'd eventually proposed, she was sure he'd done so more because he couldn't get out of it than out of a genuine desire to commit.

She wasn't going to think about it now, though. This evening was her special moment, and as they hadn't come around too often the past few years, she was going to make the most of it.

Had anyone guessed her news? Rhett had only just turned up, and although their eyes had met briefly, he'd taken a seat next to Hitch and, as they'd agreed, hadn't come over to her yet.

All eyes turned to her, and she felt oddly flustered, not her usual self at all. "Um..." She couldn't look at Rhett, whose gaze burned into her, sending shivers down her spine, and she studied her shoes. "It's just that... um... Rhett and I are... um... kind of... back together."

She lifted her gaze. Everyone's faced mirrored their surprise as they stared at her, then at Rhett, who just raised his eyebrows, then back at her. She shrugged, conscious that her face was growing warm. "What can you do?"

At that point, they all started laughing and rose to hug her and Rhett, all talking at once.

Callie shook her head, clearly bemused. "What could possibly have happened to get the two of you even talking, let alone doing anything else? I never thought I'd see you even having a conversation again."

Rhett had told Neve that he didn't want the others to know about his illness, so she just said, "I don't know, we got talking, and we cleared a few things up. And I suppose we both remembered how good we were together, and how much we'd missed each other." She looked at Callie and rolled her eyes. "Jeez. Hormones again?"

Tears trickled down Callie's cheeks. "It's just so lovely. I hated that the two of you wouldn't talk. This is wonderful."

Rhett laughed. "I'd hug you but I don't think I'd be able to get close enough."

"Doesn't stop me," Neve said, and she grabbed her friend from the side so she didn't press on her bump.

"I'm so glad," Callie whispered. They moved away a little as the others asked Rhett questions about the course they'd been on. "You're so right for each other. It made me sad that you couldn't see it."

"I was too stuck in my ways," Neve murmured back. "Too caught up in the past. He taught me how to let go, that's all."

"It sounds so simple, but I know it's not." Callie rubbed her nose. "I admire you for moving forward."

"He said sorry," Neve admitted, "and it just broke me. I don't think men realize how important the word is. I didn't make a fuss about it, but it's the first time he's actually said it. I know it doesn't mean it was all his fault—far from it. But it meant something to me that he realized he played a part, and he's sorry about it. He said that we all make mistakes, and being a grown up is about accepting that, and about forgiving. I know I'm proud and stubborn, and I bear grudges. I don't like that about myself. But I'm going to try to be better."

"You can't do more than that." Callie gave her an appraising look. "What about your dad? Will your new outlook affect your relationship with him?"

"Maybe. We're going to go and see him on Sunday." Neve hesitated. "Rhett wants to come with me, and I want him there—I do want to tell them we're back together—but I'm worried that if Dad changes his opinion, he'll only do it because he thinks we're going steady. Does that make sense? I want him to accept me for who I am, not who he thinks I am."

Callie tipped her head from side to side. "I know what you mean, but ultimately, sweetie, what does it matter? In the perfect world, all men would accept that a woman can have numerous partners the same as a guy without it making them a slut, but unfortunately we're a long way from that. I doubt you'll be able to change your dad's view no matter how hard you try. You have to remember that just because someone says something, it doesn't make it so."

"I guess." Neve hadn't thought of it like that.

"If it pleases him to think you're 'settling down,'" and Callie put air quotes around the words, "then why not let him? I get frustrated when I see us all trying to please our parents as we grow up. Sometimes I envy Hitch, and that's a terrible thing to say and you know I don't mean it, but it must be nice not feeling as if your folks are looking over your shoulder the whole time."

"Yeah, I know what you mean. Why do we always want approval? We're grown-ups, aren't we?"

Callie tipped her hand from side to side, and Neve laughed.

"You're right, though," Callie said. "We are grown-ups, and we're past the stage where we need our parents to approve everything we do. We should be able to choose to live our lives however we want—to marry whom we choose, to bring our kids up in our own way. I've got that battle coming—I can see it from a mile away." She rested a hand on her bump, her brow creasing with frustration."

"Maybe we should make a pact now, to stick to our guns," Neve said, "and to live our lives the way we want."

"Yeah, lets."

They walked back to the table and picked up their glasses as they sat.

"I'd like to make a toast," Neve said. Everyone picked up his or her glass. "To living our lives the way we want."

She could see on the faces of the men and women around the table that the phrase meant something to each of them. Strange, she thought as she sipped her wine, that we let other people influence us so much. Callie was right—just because Neve's father had called her a slut didn't make it so. There was nothing wrong with liking sex, and nothing wrong with having had a few partners along the way, as long as both parties were adults and consenting, and they used protection. Where was the harm in it? Sex was nice, she thought, and sharing your body with someone else was fun.

Her gaze slid across to Rhett. She wasn't surprised to find him watching her. He winked, and they exchanged a secret smile that gave her a tingle down her spine. Whatever happened with her father, she would be going home with Rhett, tonight and hopefully every night from now until the end of her days. She had to concentrate on that, and hope that it would give her strength to cope with whatever life brought her.

*

On Sunday, Neve and Rhett arrived at her parents' house just before one o'clock.

"I can't believe you talked me into going for lunch," she grumbled as she rang the doorbell. "It's like going out on a first date—you never go for a meal in case you want to make a quick escape."

He chuckled and held her hand. "Eating also gives you something else to do if the conversation isn't going well."

"That's a good point."

"Not that it won't be," he added. "It's going to be fine."

Neve didn't say anything. Her stomach was knotted like an old ball of wool. She'd barely slept the night before, even though Rhett had done his best to wear her out. After a lovely, relaxed evening spent watching a movie while they ate nachos with chili, salsa, and sour cream, and shared a tub of chocolate fudge brownie ice cream, they'd spent a just-as-delicious time in bed rediscovering each other at their leisure, kissing and touching for ages before they eventually gave in to their desire.

Rhett had fallen asleep quickly, but Neve had lain awake long into the night, listening to his breathing, loving having him beside her, but unable to sleep nevertheless.

Now her eyes felt scratchy, her mood on the edge of irritable. She was tempted to turn around and go home, but Rhett's hand was tight on hers, and she'd promised him she'd at least try to make it work.

"You need this," he'd said to her before he'd fallen asleep. "I know you well enough to know that you need to make peace with your father, even if it's an uneasy one. Do it for me."

It had reminded her that he didn't have a father anymore, and it had made her so sad that she'd promised to try.

So she took a deep breath and pinned a smile on her face as the door opened.

Bella Clark answered it, her look of hope morphing into delight as she saw that her eldest daughter had actually turned up. Throwing her arms around Neve, she squeezed her tightly before drawing back and looking up with pleasure at the man standing by her side.

"Deana said you were coming. It's so lovely to see you again, Rhett."

"It's very kind of you to invite me to lunch, Mrs. Clark."

"Oh, Bella, please. Let's start off on the right foot. Come in, come in."

Her heart racing, Neve passed by her mother and walked along the corridor and into the living room. Deana and Jamie were already there, sitting on the sofa with Lara, their little girl, while Deana nursed the baby. Brian Clark stood by the window, looking out onto the road, so he must have seen them arrive.

He turned as they walked in. Neve ignored him for a moment, hugged Jamie, then Lara, and bent to kiss Deana and then the baby. Rhett followed behind her, shaking hands with Jamie and kissing the girls.

Finally, Neve turned to her father. She couldn't have prepared herself for this even if she'd wanted to. The last time she'd seen him, he'd basically called her a whore. Even with all her promises to Rhett and her aim to move on, she didn't know if she could ever forgive him for that.

People make mistakes. Including you. Adults realize this, and adults can forgive each other when they do it. They'd been wise words. But now she was in front of her father, looking into his eyes, Neve knew that she wouldn't be able to forgive him, not unless he admitted his part in the problem. She'd been able to forgive Rhett because he'd said sorry, and she needed the same from her father.

She swallowed hard. "Hi, Dad."

"Hello." His blue eyes were icy, hard. But then so were hers, she thought, and she hated it when people said she was cold.

She bit her lip, emotion making her speechless. Why was this so difficult? She wanted to scream like a toddler, throw something, hammer her fists on his chest. But she was an adult, and she was supposed to stop acting like a child.

Behind her, Rhett cleared his throat. "Hello, Mr. Clark. It's nice to see you again."

Brian's gaze slid to Rhett, and a genuine smile curved his lips. "Hello, lad." He held out his hand, and Rhett shook it. "So... the two of you are dating again, are you?"

Rhett glanced at her, obviously saw she was tongue-tied, and nodded. "Just started. It's been a while, but we bumped into each other in Queenstown and got talking, and I remembered what an amazing girl your daughter is."

Brian's gaze came back to her, and his expression softened. "Yes, she is. And she's just as stubborn and feisty as her old dad."

"Peas from a pod," Rhett said. He took her hand again by her side, his skin warm on hers, and squeezed her fingers.

"Is it a long-term thing?" Brian wanted to know.

Neve bristled and opened her mouth, inches away from snapping *That's none of your fucking business and what a fucking awful thing to say to the man I've just started dating.*

But Rhett said, "Well, I'd propose now but I know she's been looking for a man as wonderful as her father, so I guess I'll have to wait a while to see whether I'll live up to her high standards." His pleasant tone nevertheless held an edge.

She inhaled, his words blowing her away. In one smooth sentence he'd implied the reason she'd not settled yet was because none of the guys she'd dated were as good to her as her dad—a flattering gesture to his future father-in-law. He'd also told Brian that he knew about his comment, and she wondered whether her father had picked up his subtle, almost indistinguishable warning that he didn't like it.

Her father's look turned wry, but he just gave a small nod, almost of approval.

She rubbed her nose, feeling as if she were five again. What could she say to wipe away the memory of her dad's awful words? And why did she care so much?

"It's been a while," Brian said.

"You hurt my feelings, Dad." She couldn't stop herself saying it. She couldn't stand there and gloss over it as if it hadn't happened. Did it make her a terrible person? She wanted to change, and yet maybe she couldn't alter that part of her.

"Seems to me perhaps we should declare a truce," Brian said softly. "Some things were said last time that shouldn't have been said. Can't turn back the clock, but maybe we can begin again, eh?"

It was so close to what Rhett had said about starting each day afresh that emotion rushed through her, and her bottom lip trembled. She lifted her chin and nodded, and Brian held out his arms.

Rhett released her hand, and she walked up to her father and hugged him.

Behind her, she heard her mother breathe out a sigh of relief. "Okay, that's good. Lunch is ready everyone. Come and sit at the table."

Neve listened to Rhett talking to Jamie about the rugby as they walked over and took their seats; she heard Deana telling Lara to sit nicely at the table; heard her mother offering portions of Shepherd's Pie and ever-so-cheerfully discussing the weather, which meant she was trying to hide her own emotion.

"I'm sorry," her father whispered, so softly she almost missed it.

She buried her face in his chest, let his arms tighten around her, and finally let go of the past.

Epilogue

It often rained in October, but not like this. Torrents poured, covering the roads with sheets of water, and lightning flashed periodically, tearing apart the dull spring sky.

Neve met Rhett's gaze, and she pulled an *eek* face. "Jeez. Poor Birdie."

His brow furrowed as he slowed the car to drive through a huge puddle. "Shame you can't book the weather for a wedding too."

"Yeah."

"I wonder if she's glad now that she's having a small do. It would be worse if she had a few hundred guests and a big church wedding, wouldn't it?"

"I suppose." Neve looked out of the window, at the people walking through the streets of Wellington with their collars turned up against the rain and cold wind.

Out of the corner of her eye, she saw Rhett glance at her. He reached out and held her hand. "Are you still worried about her?"

"Sort of."

"She'll be all right. I know it's supposed to be the most important day of your life but that's bullshit really, isn't it? Surely the weather and the food and everything else is irrelevant?"

"There speaks a true Kiwi man," she said, amused.

"Mock all you like—the important thing is that the guy she loves is about to commit himself to her for the rest of his life."

"That's what worries me."

He sighed. "I know you don't like Mal, but he's the one she's chosen, so you're just going to have to put up with him."

"I know." Neve stared moodily out of the window.

Rhett laughed. "Don't sulk. One of your best friends is getting married. You should be dancing in the aisles."

"There won't be any aisles. She's getting married in a registry office."

"It was a figure of speech," he said, amused. "Come on, out with it. What's the matter?"

"I don't want to tell you. You'll laugh."

"Maybe. You should tell me anyway."

She shrugged. "I know I was raised a Catholic, but I don't consider myself religious. In spite of that, though, I do value marriage. I don't think it should be entered into lightly. I think that's the purpose behind the pomp and ceremony—it's to remind those taking their vows how important they are."

He drew up at a T junction and turned interested eyes on her. "I didn't realize you felt like that."

"Well, I do, and you can mock all you like."

"Why would I mock you?"

"Because everyone thinks I'm hard-nosed and unromantic."

He turned the car left. "This is me you're talking to. I think you're one of the most romantic people I know."

"What?"

"Oh, come on. You might not wear skirts and have ribbons in your hair, but you love chick flicks, soppy romance novels, puppies, babies… Need I go on? You're like one of those caramel chocolates you bite into thinking they're going to be hard and chewy, but they turn out to be soft and gooey on the inside. So tell me, what's the problem with Birdie and Mal?"

He always did that—said something unexpected and lovely to make her head spin, and then carried on talking.

"It's not a problem," she said, trying to gather her wits. "It's just that, like I said, in my view marriage isn't to be entered into lightly. And I feel that they're both half-hearted about it."

"You think them choosing to have a small wedding means they're half-hearted?"

"No. I think small weddings can be beautiful, and I definitely wouldn't want a huge flouncy affair. It'd frighten the crap out of me. But it's as if Birdie gave Mal an ultimatum—to commit to her or she'd leave him—and he said yeah okay, so they booked the registry office and threw a party together. I'm not bothered that she doesn't have bridesmaids or anything—I don't think you have to have fuss to make it a lovely day—but I can't help but think that deep down she wants that. You know Birdie, she's all frills and fancy. She wants the big white dress and the walking down the aisle and the celebration,

I'm certain of it. But neither of them has been acting as if it's the best day of their life, as if they can't wait to take their vows, you know?"

Rhett signaled and pulled up on the roadside, reversed into a space, and turned off the engine. He unclipped his seatbelt, and she did the same and went to get out of the car, but he stopped her with a hand on her arm.

She turned to face him, thinking how lovely he looked today. He wore a dark suit with a white shirt and a silvery-gray tie. He'd taken time over his hair and wore a gorgeous aftershave. He looked lovely enough to have for lunch.

There was also a look in his eye that gave her goose bumps.

"What?" she asked, puzzled.

"I didn't expect this," he said. "I'm unprepared."

"For what?" Now she was confused.

"What you just said—it made me lightheaded. It made my heart race."

"What did I say?" Now she felt alarmed.

"That you think getting married is about not being able to wait to take your vows. You sound as if you think a wedding should be exciting."

"It should be, if you really love someone. Shouldn't it?"

"Marry me," he said. "Let me tell everyone you're going to be mine for the rest of your life."

Her eyes widened and she stared at him. "What?"

He reached out a hand and tucked her hair behind her ear. "I don't care how you want to do it. We can have a thousand guests and a huge white dress and get married in church. Or we can elope to Fiji or Scotland or Antarctica and it just be the two of us. Whatever we do, it'll be a magical day for me. I feel excited to think about being married to you, Neve. I want you to wear my ring. I want the world to know you're taken. Say yes."

Her breath caught in her throat, and then a smile spread across her face. "Yes! Of course I'll marry you. Oh Rhett." She threw her arms around him and hugged him tightly. "Oh jeez, why do you do this to me? I can't cry—my mascara will run."

"I don't care," he said fiercely. "You'll always be the most beautiful woman I've ever seen, no matter if you have eyes like a panda. I want you. I want to marry you. I want to have kids. I want to be with you forever."

"Oh for God's sake stop or I'm going to start bawling like a five-year-old."

He laughed, took her face in his hands, and kissed her. She mumbled that he was going to kiss off her lipstick, but he didn't stop, just kissed her until she went limp and sagged against him, and then he kissed her some more.

They only stopped when someone banged on the window. Rhett looked over his shoulder and laughed, then lowered it to reveal Hitch's face.

"You're steaming up the windows," Hitch said, using a newspaper to shield his head from the rain. "It's indecent, and Birdie's here. Get a fucking move on."

Rhett gave him the finger and raised the window, and Neve laughed.

"We'd better go," she said, fishing her lipstick out of her bag.

"Wait a minute." He grabbed her for a final kiss. "I love you."

"I love you too." She couldn't believe how right it felt to say that. How could she ever have thought she could live without him?

"Come on then." He let her reapply her lipstick, then put a hand on the door handle. "Ready?"

They dashed out into the rain, Neve squealing, and held hands as they ran to join their friends.

*

Read Bridget's story in Persuading Spring, The Four Seasons Book 4

The Four Seasons

Book 1: Seducing Summer
Book 2: Tempting Autumn
Book 3: Bewitching Winter
Book 4: Persuading Spring

If you'd like to be informed when my next book is available, you can sign up for my mailing list on my website, http://www.serenitywoodsromance.com

I also send exclusive short stories and sometimes free books!

About the Author

Serenity Woods lives in the sub-tropical Northland of New Zealand with her wonderful husband and gorgeous teenage son. She writes hot and sultry contemporary romances, and she would much rather immerse herself in reading or writing romance than do the dusting and ironing, which is why it's not a great idea to pop round if you have any allergies.

Website: http://www.serenitywoodsromance.com
Facebook: http://www.facebook.com/serenitywoodsromance
Twitter: https://twitter.com/Serenity_Woods

Printed in Great Britain
by Amazon